## ACCLAIM FOR AARON PATTERSON

"I would recommend this book to anyone who likes *James Patterson* or books like his. I can't wait for the next book to come out."

*—Sandra Labella, Amazon reviewer*

"...I think if *Tom Clancy* crossed genres it would look something like this. Well done."

*—Roy Bartle*

"Looking for the perfect last minute gift for the avid reader on your list...I suggest BREAKING STEELE fast paced and one of the best books I've read this year. So pleased that this is going to be a series...the writing is terrific and the characters come to life. After reading BREAKING STEELE go back to the author page and grab EVERYTHING he's written...you won't be sorry."

*—M.J. Weineburg*

# TWISTING
# STEELE

*Aaron Patterson*

StoneHouse Ink 2013
StoneHouse Ink
Boise, ID 83713
http://www.stonehouseink.net

First eBook Edition: 2013
First Paperback Edition: 2013

ISBN 978-1624820342

The characters and events portrayed in this book are fictitious. Any similarity to a real person, living or dead, is coincidental and not intended by the author. Twisting Steele: a novel by Aaron Patterson

Cover design by © Cory Clubb
Layout design by Ross Burck – rossburck@gmail.com

Creative Edit by Ellie Ann

Published in the United States of America
StoneHouse Ink

*For Kale, you are my little man. I am proud to be your father.*

# TWISTING
# STEELE

*Some lives twist together making an unbreakable cord, others choke the life out of something beautiful.*

# CHAPTER 1

I LEANED BACK WITH a small smile. The airplane seats felt more like steel wool than wool fabric and smelled like mothballs and bad breath, but I didn't care. I was going on my first vacation.

Well, technically, it was the second. But I'd hardly call the camping trip my dad took me on when I was eight—and he was drunk, or fishing (or both), the entire time—a vacation. It was more like a punishment. My family wasn't exactly the Disney-dream-vacation type. We were more like the Denny's-buffet type.

My best friend, Mandy, sat next to me, scribbling a list on her field notebook. She had it braced against her knee because we were about to take off and couldn't put down the table.

"What are you—?"

"Shhh," Mandy cut me off. She wrote so quickly I expected her pen to start smoking. "Just … one … more … thing. All right." She looked up with a smile and handed me the notebook. "There it is. Our to-do list for Rio."

My eyes trailed the list and then my mouth hung open as I turned the page. There had to be at least fifty items on it.

*- Get palm trees painted on my nails.*

*- Go scuba diving and get a picture with a red fish.*

*- Flirt with my scuba instructor, but not so badly that he asks me for my number—just enough that I can say I did it.*

*- Get Sarah a date with our scuba instructor.*

*- Have a conversation with a parrot.*

*- Go shopping and MAKE Sarah get some new clothes.*

*- Eat a huge lobster dinner. Wear a giant bib.*

*- Race a bike through the streets of Rio.*

*- Go surfing and try to ride at least one wave. If I can't, at least get a picture of me standing on a surfboard so I can tell Rick I did, because he's never been surfing.*

*- Not get eaten by sharks.*

*- Solve a mystery.*

*- Get a glow-in-the-dark bikini and go swimming at night.*

*- Get a tattoo of a typewriter on my back.*

*- Read War and Peace. And the latest Janet Evanovich to balance it out.*

*- Adopt an orphaned street kid.*

I didn't get through half the list before I broke into laughter. "You'd think we were planning to be in Rio eleven years, not eleven days." I combed my hand through my blonde hair. "And haven't I told you a thousand times not to talk to parrots you don't know?"

"You're so biased—you always let me talk to dogs. Hey, we've got to fit as much as we can into this vacation. This may be the only chance we ever get to do this." Mandy clicked and unclicked her pen, a nervous habit. She wasn't crazy about planes.

I took the pen from her. "Why? Are you and Rick going to start popping out babies soon?"

She patted her flat belly. "My chances are drying up as we speak."

I wrinkled my nose.

She leaned in and her curly red hair brushed my cheek. "But really, we've talked about doing this our whole lives. And now we've made it happen."

"*You* made it happen," I said. "If you hadn't forced me to buy a ticket at water-gun point, I'd be sitting at my desk at the office going through case files with Dan trying to look down my shirt."

My boss, District Attorney Dan Butler, was less than discreet about one of the reasons why he wanted me on his payroll.

She squinted in mock sternness. "No one can say no to my water gun. And, you're welcome."

My face softened. I wanted to tell her how just how glad I was to be taking this trip with her. But she'd probably get all mushy on me, something my crusty old soul tried to avoid.

I tapped her list. "What's with this entry? You don't even like kids."

"Not true. Rick and I would love a few ankle-biters around the house. What I hate are spoiled brats who order their parents around like slaves. I bet I'd like a Rio street kid."

"You might be suited for each other … both orphans, with dubious moral standards and personal hygiene—"

"Hey." She punched my arm. "So I forget to wear deodorant one time at the gym and you're going to tease me forever?"

I rubbed the spot where she hit me. "One time at the gym? Try all of eighth grade."

Mandy shook her head, and her smile faded. "Those are the important things moms are supposed to teach you. 'Put on deodorant or you'll smell like a fish tank.'"

My phone buzzed. Oops. It was supposed to be off already. I

awkwardly dug it out of my back pocket, trying not to elbow Mandy in the ribs, and checked the screen. I turned my shoulder and kept the phone low to block the flight attendant's view.

"Is it Solomon?" Mandy asked. She took out her phone—it's impossible not to check your phone if someone else is. "I'd better text Rick."

My face grew wooden when I saw the screen. UNKNOWN. Those calls were never good. It buzzed two more times before I braced myself enough to answer.

"Hello?"

A recorded female voice said in robotic tones, "You are getting a collect call from—"

And then a voice said my name, a voice that I hadn't heard in ten years—ever since the trial—my mom's. "Sarah? Baby? Hi. It's Mom. Please take my call. I know we ended the last visit badly, but since it's your birthday, I wanted to hear your voice. Please. You owe it to me—"

That's when I hung up. Already my heart was beating so fast I felt my temple pulsing. Her words burned. It was all wrong. So wrong. Why did she have to do everything so wrong?

"Who was that?" Mandy asked quietly.

"Mom."

I couldn't talk over the anger simmering in my chest.

After taking a jerky breath, I said, "She called to wish me a happy birthday."

Mandy's eyebrows creased in confusion. "But your birthday is the fifteenth of—"

"Next month." I gripped my phone so hard its frame clicked. I set it down before I broke it.

Mandy winced. "How could a mom forget her own kid's birthday?"

That question, and questions like it, had hounded me the first twenty-five years of my life. The worst part of it was—she thought she was a good mom and everything was my fault. She had such a twisted view of things.

"I'm sure the few good brain cells she has left are used to con smokes off people in prison, not remember my birthday."

I took a deep breath and looked around at the flight attendants combing the aisles, making sure everything was in place before takeoff.

Mom couldn't do this to me, couldn't break into my life and ruin it without me letting her in first. She'd done enough already. I turned my phone off and slipped it in my purse. Mandy must have recognized it as the end of the subject and took out her book. That's one reason I liked her—she let things go.

The airplane started to taxi down the runway, lumbering loudly across the lot. How could something so graceful in the air be so awkward on land?

Mandy put her book down and gripped the armrest. "What'd you bring to read at the beach?" she said in a high-pitched voice.

She was using the distraction technique on herself, so I took out the thick book I'd brought. "It's *Blunt Trauma Injuries* by—"

"Oh, God, Sarah," Mandy interrupted me. "You have no idea how to go on a vacation, do you?"

"Don't mock me. I like learning about bruises and how to tell how old they are. Did you know that—" I stopped.

She was so pale her freckles stood out even more than usual.

Poor thing. I tried to reassure her. "You know it's more dangerous to ride in a car than a plane, right?"

"Irrational fears are called irrational for a reason." She gritted her teeth. "It's normal. I'm normal. 72% of people are afraid of flying."

"And 34.5% of statistics are made up on the spot." I rested my head against the seat and closed my eyes. Then Mandy started doing the thing she did incessantly when she was scared—she chattered.

"So what do you want to do in Rio? It's your first time on the beach. I hope you brought your orange bikini instead of your yellow one. I told you to make a list. What do you want to do? You always make me do the planning—why don't you have a plan for this vacation? Don't you care about it?"

I looked over with heavy-lidded eyes. "Lists are your thing, not mine. My one goal for this vacation is to sleep in until ten."

Sleep had never been my friend. A side of me came out at night that I tried to push away. Memories came unbidden, like evil sheep demanding to be counted—thoughts of my dad, my mom, that tragic day twelve years ago, the recent trauma I'd encountered at the hands of the murderer and kidnapper, Hank Williams, the night I killed him—the scenes played over and over again so that sleep was impossible.

"That's it? That's all you want out of our trip?" Mandy said. I glared at her. "Oh, right. Okay, then. I'll let you sleep in."

The airplane gained speed.

"But not every day." She gulped loudly. "Maybe once."

I gazed past her to the window. The land rushed past. That would be enough—I'd sing the Hallelujah Chorus if I just got to sleep in once.

The 737 lifted off the ground. I loved the way the speed of the airplane forced me back into my seat, loved the power and the pure lack of control I had to have in order to trust that we wouldn't end up in a ball of flames on the tarmac.

Mandy shot me a scared glance. "I need air and water… can I get a drink of water? My legs hurt. I have to go to the bathroom."

"As soon as we level off, I'm sure you can get a drink and go potty." My gut turned as we lifted off.

"'Go potty'? Who says 'go potty'? What are you, four?" Mandy gritted her teeth and squeezed her eyes shut.

"I can say 'potty' if I want. I mean, in a few minutes we're going to die as the wings tear off and we plummet to the ground. I can hear the screams now…"

"I hate you. I can't believe you're teasing me at a time like this. You are teasing me, right?" Mandy stared at me with big, dark eyes and a pleading look.

"Well …" Leaning over her, I looked out the window and pretended to survey the stability of the wings. "Everything looks okay from here. No sign of the airplane socket mites responsible for most crashes. We should be okay as long as we don't hit a flock of geese."

Mandy cursed. "How long till we're in Rio?"

I gave her a blank look. "We just left Boise."

That's when I realized I'd be very lucky if I slept at all this vacation.

# CHAPTER 2

COLD METAL PRESSED AGAINST the side of Nancy Parker's head and her bladder released, soiling her Gucci sable dress. Her hands were cuffed to the wheel. The woman holding the gun to Nancy's head was an unnatural blonde, with light brown skin, black painted nails, and a sunburnt nose.

"You just pissed yourself?" Her voice was calm, with a hint of an accent. "Look, all you have to do is sit here with me, look out the window, and enjoy Rio's beautiful ocean view. I told you that I wouldn't kill you if you do exactly what I say."

Nancy shifted in her seat, and the woman lowered the gun and laid it on her lap. "See, now we can relax." Pushing her sunglasses up with her middle finger, she turned and blew smoke out of the tiny crack between the window and the frame of the car. Not that it did much good. The car was clouded in pungent smoke, making it hard for Nancy to breathe.

Nancy cursed her own vanity. She'd been shopping for a scarf—something to go with the dress she'd wear to dinner. Her friend had offered to go with her, but she'd told him to continue watching the soccer game. She'd only be a minute. As she'd crossed the street to the shopping area, a car had stopped in front of her, a gun had pointed at her face, and a girl had shoved her into the vehicle from behind.

Now they were parked on the outskirts of town in an abandoned plastic factory parking lot. It was littered with trash, a shanty stood in the corner with a homeless person sleeping beside it, and a dead puppy lay next to him.

Nancy shivered. She'd never been this frightened. Her voice shook and tears welled up in her eyes. "Please ... you can have everything. My husband's rich, very rich. Just let me go. Do you *entende*?"

Snatching the gun up, the blonde ground it into Nancy's ribs, making her cry out in pain. "Shut up, *vadia*. All you filthy-rich women are the same—none of you earned the money you have. You go whoring yourself out to men—not only your own men, but also other women's men. I HATE YOU ALL," she screamed the last words. "I have to sit here in a stinking lot, smelling your piss and your fear, and listen to your whining. Keep it up and I will kill you just to get some peace and quiet."

Nancy bit her lip, clenched her jaw, and willed herself not to cry. Sweat soaked her back and she gripped the steering wheel.

"That's better." Placing the gun back in her lap, the woman smiled. She looked like a bug in her oversized sunglasses. "This takes two hours at the most. It's been an hour. See, hon, we're halfway there." Her tone went from violently angry to chipper in a split second. "I guess I'm willing to do anything for money too, as long as it doesn't involve taking orders from a man."

Nancy stared out at the ocean just beyond the parking lot and past the winding concrete path. There was no help coming for her.

"I like this time of the year. Flowers blooming, babies everywhere, sunlight lasting through the evening, warm sand, everyone running around half naked." Nancy's kidnapper seemed to lose her train of thought as if tangled in a long-forgotten memory.

She paused, and then said with a sigh, "You know, when I was a little girl I used to lay on the beach in my little bikini. My mama hated it, said I would attract the wrong kind of guy." She laughed. "She should have been scared for the guys. My *avó* understood. She called me a *borboleta*, a butterfly, said I'd have great delight in fluttering around in beautiful wings, sipping the nectar of life, not caring a flitter or flutter about anyone else, and then die young, with great joy."

Nancy let her shoulders relax and she took a deep breath. Maybe she could get through to the woman, make conversation and somehow get out of this alive. "Do you have any siblings?"

In a flash of silver, the gun whipped across her cheek. Bright white flooded her vision and pain exploded down her face and neck. Again, the hard metal handgun crashed into her face.

Nancy twisted and pulled, trying to dodge the blows, but it was no use. She was trapped and couldn't shield herself.

She wasn't aware of when the beating stopped, just that her head was down. She watched blood drip off the tip of her nose and splatter on her pale pink dress.

"Don't try that again." Breathing hard, her captor coughed and cursed. "The next time you try to work me, I'll put a bullet in your head." She swallowed, and then spoke as if to herself. "*Puta que pariu.* What's taking them so long?"

# CHAPTER 3

I SOAKED IN THE sight of Rio. A thousand shades of green covered towering cliffs that rose around the city. Palm trees lined every street, their leaves rustling in the hot wind. On the shuttle ride from the airport to our hotel, we passed skyscrapers and gleaming shopping malls, dirty marketplaces and crowded tenements. But my eyes kept pulling back to the ocean. It would be my first visit to the beach, and I was thirsty for the experience.

The hotel Mandy had reserved was simple and clean, nothing lavish, but very tastefully put together. It smelled of coconuts and tanning oil, with a hint of fresh fish. Not smelly, oily fish, but the clean, white fish I loved to eat. The hotel beside it, some Hilton or another, dwarfed it both in size and opulence. I was glad Mandy had chosen this local hotel—it had more character. We might as well be in the States if we stayed in a Hilton.

I took one of the complimentary hard candies at the counter as Mandy checked in. It was strawberry, my favorite. I suddenly remembered I hadn't turned on my phone since getting off the airplane. Even though it had cost me a pretty penny, I'd decided to spring for the international phone plan that month just so I could stay in contact with …

Ah. Two messages from Solomon. I read them both twice, a small smile tugging at my lips.

*Have a safe flight. Don't forget about me and fall for some hot beach bum.*

*Thinking about you.*

It was a small thing, but it made me feel good. Besides our weekly gun training class, I'd gone out with him a few times and we texted a lot. Our outings couldn't even be called dates, and I was glad about that. I liked relationships to move at tortoise speed. That, paired with the fact that I wouldn't sleep with any guys I didn't trust wholeheartedly (a whopping total of two men) and my all-consuming career, I usually landed in the department of "not worth the hassle." But Solomon had seen something in me, and I liked him back. I enjoyed his humor, his confidence, and the fact that he wasn't needy. He liked to have me around, but didn't hound me.

He did draw a few red flags. I thought he must work for the government or something—out of the nine times we'd gone out, five times he'd received a phone call and left at a moment's notice. Plus, when I'd Googled him, there was absolutely nothing on him. Even regular Joes leave a little cyber trail, but his was hidden, which made me think CIA. But maybe it also meant that I had an overactive imagination and a weakness for spies.

I asked him once what he did and he gave me a nondescript answer. "I work with my cousin as a consultant." Whatever that meant. I had a dating rule: never get involved with anyone in the legal system. That meant no cops, FBI, CIA, lawyers, judges, and so on. It was hard enough *working* in the system with my past, let alone *date* in it.

I texted back. *Just arrived. Met a cute beach bum. Getting married at 4. Now I need to learn Portuguese.*

My phone instantly buzzed back. *Mazel tov. Language is overrated.*

As I tried to think of a good comeback, he texted again. Whoa. It was more like a novel.

*Hey, watch out. Micro-kidnappers called the Blondes like to take ladies and empty their bank accounts. Don't go anywhere alone. And don't act rich.*

I texted back. *Shouldn't be hard since I'm not rich. Thanks for the warning. How'd a consultant know what criminals to watch for in Rio?*

*I Google.*

*Try again.*

*I work for the FBI.*

My jaw tightened. I saw that Mandy was done at the desk. I slipped my phone back in my purse with a shake of my head, following the bellhop who'd stacked our luggage on her cart. Was he joking? I had no patience with men who lied.

I didn't want to ruin my vacation right off, so I decided I would talk to Solomon later and find out why he'd dodged me.

Our room had two double beds with deep goose-down comforters and luxurious red silk sheets peeping from underneath the covers. I went straight to my bed and slid my hand along it, feeling the softness, and then squeezed the pillow. Ah. Just right. If I were able to sleep in, that bed would do it for me.

The bellhop unloaded our bags with great care. I studied her from the corner of my eye. She was moving slowly, as if sore. Her arm, from the shoulder to the elbow, was covered in welts and bruises— some swollen and plum purple, others yellowed with age. I would have given her the benefit of the doubt until she craned her neck sideways and I noticed the hickeys on her collarbone. Her nametag said "Lucy." She looked strong and athletic, not a likely victim. My eyes lowered in sadness. There was no way to escape from the evils of the world—not even on vacation.

I gave her an extra ten bucks, which she accepted with downcast eyes. I noticed Mandy also slipping her something extra—she must've seen the bruises as well.

After Lucy left, I flung myself on the bed and melted into the cloud-like comforter. I'd rested, like, three seconds before Mandy tugged at my ankle. I cracked my eyes open. She wore her bright green bikini.

"Whaa—?" I rolled my eyes. "Were you wearing that under your clothes?"

"No." She laughed, wrapping a towel around her hips. "Let's go to the beach. Don't you want to feel the sand between your toes?"

A slow smile spread across my face. I'd been looking forward to this moment my whole life.

# CHAPTER 4

I PUSHED MY TOES into the sand and lay back in the short beach chair. The ocean crashed not ten feet from us and the smell of the sea cleared my mind. Boise seemed like another world. The sun melted the stress of the journey away and I let out a long sigh.

"I agree." Mandy's sigh was just as long.

I looked over at her and smirked, glad I wore sunglasses—Mandy's pale skin was blinding. "We've been out in the sun for twenty minutes, Snow White. I think you need to reapply your sunscreen."

"Just because I'm a redhead doesn't mean I can't tan. If I lay out every day wearing SPF 50, by the end of summer I will start to get some color."

I took a sip of my lemon drop martini. "Yeah ... you'll be *red*."

Mandy grunted and sipped her drink. She wore a huge white hat that could shade a whole football team.

I looked at the ocean, letting the sunrays wash over me, listening to children splashing in the waves and the sound of gulls. My mind wandered.

"Whatcha thinkin'?" Mandy propped herself on her elbow.

I could feel the alcohol hitting my head. "Dang, these drinks are strong."

"That's not an answer, and yes, they don't make 'em like this in Boise."

"Hmm, what am I thinking? Solomon, my life, Angela, and ADA work."

Mandy snorted. "Whatever. You're only thinking about Solomon—you just added in the other stuff so you don't seem like an obsessive, love-struck little girl."

"Dangit, Mandy, we know each other too well. It's not even fun anymore."

"It's fun for me." Mandy accepted a fresh drink from a dark-skinned shirtless guy with perfect abs, and smiled up at him. As he walked away, she said, "I love this hotel."

"I know. The room is clean and the breakfast bar looks incredible."

"I was talking about the hot shirtless guys." She winked at the waiter when he looked back.

Mandy was good for the soul. She made life more fun, and at times she was the only thing that kept me from going crazy. I knew I could always count on her and her disjointed humor. She didn't even know how much I relied on her.

"So how's Angela doing?"

Angela was one of the girls I trained at an inner-city kickboxing gym. She'd been kidnapped by Hank Williams as a way to get to me. I still felt a rush of guilt every time I thought about it.

"She's good, as good as can be expected. I've been training with her a lot and her kickboxing is really improving. She refused to go to counseling, which worries me. She keeps what happened to herself, but I think she's working out a lot of her feelings in training."

"I feel bad for her. No one should have to go through what she did." Mandy turned to me and scanned my body up and down. "And I must say, kickboxing agrees with you." She changed subjects faster than a toddler changes moods.

My cheeks flushed and I looked down at my smooth belly. It was dotted with sweat under the warm sun. I changed the subject, uncomfortable with body evaluation. "Angela's teaching the class till I get back. I think it'll be good for her."

Mandy nodded. "Yeah, the other girls really look up to her."

I stood and breathed in deeply. The water was calling me. "Ready to hit the waves?"

She shook her head. "Not on your life. I'm too busy drinking and napping."

I laughed. "What about your list of a thousand things to do?"

"I'll get started on it tonight."

"Procrastinator."

A smile spread across Mandy's face. "Mmmhmm."

I walked toward the ocean and someone whistled. I turned to see a tan, dark-haired man grinning at me from down the beach. I smiled and kept walking.

The water was surprisingly warm. Waves hit my feet and washed out, making me sink in the sand a little more with each splash. I walked out farther and when the water was up to my waist, I dove in and lost myself in the joy of the ocean.

# CHAPTER 5

"PLEASE LET ME GO. You have my purse, so you don't need me. I won't tell anyone, I swear."

Vitoria cursed and pulled on her cigarette. She thought about quitting smokes for the tenth time and quickly dismissed the idea. How else would she deal with her stressful job?

"Calm down now—everything will be fine. You sit there, I sit here, and when I get a phone call from my friends, I'll let you go."

The woman, Nancy Parker, sobbed, causing her mascara to run down her cheeks. "But why keep me? I won't do anything—"

Vitoria twisted in her seat, rage filling her, making her lose all self-control. She ground her cigarette into the woman's arm and held it there as she writhed and screamed. The handcuffs kept her from getting away. A smile took the corner of Vitoria's mouth.

"Ohmygod, please—" The woman yanked so hard that the cuffs broke the skin on her wrists and the steering wheel creaked under the pressure. She hit the horn and kicked the floor. It was like having a rabbit on the end of a snare. She was going to hurt herself if she kept it up.

Vitoria's phone buzzed, and she answered it as she threw the collapsed cigarette stub out the window. "Yeah?"

Nancy moaned and trembled, hanging her head as if she was about to faint.

"We've taken all we can from her accounts," said the female voice on the other end of the line. She was the only rich female Vitoria had ever met and not hated. "Now we need the password to her account in Copenhagen."

Vitoria put the mouthpiece of the phone to her shoulder. "What's the password to your bank account in Copenhagen?"

Nancy's face was swollen and red and she gasped for breath, her nose running.

"Well?" Vitoria said, her voice rising in anger.

"It's mountfuji79800216chapter."

Not a bad password. Most passwords were the name of their dogs and date of birth. Vitoria repeated it to her contact. Nancy hid her face in the crook of her elbow, muffling her sobs.

"Anything else?" Vitoria asked.

"No." *Click*.

Time to finish the job the way she'd always wanted to. She knew it would change her forever, but she was ready for it. After taking a quick breath, she drew a .22. It had a silencer attached to the barrel. She jacked a round into the chamber and fired twice into Nancy's head.

The gunshot was nothing more than a *pop*, as .22s didn't make much noise even without a silencer. Blood splattered the driver's side window and the woman slumped forward.

Flipping open her cell, Vitoria texted Mia to come pick her up. The gang would probably be wondering about Nancy, but they wouldn't ask any questions. *Vitoria* was the only one who could ask questions. Once they found out about Nancy's death, they'd be mad at her. At first. Then they'd come around. No one could say no to the kind of money they'd be earning.

Vitoria took out another cigarette and flicked her lighter. She looked out over the city and opened the door. It was a beautiful day, hot and humid—just how she liked it.

She left the abandoned parking lot. Nothing was flat in Rio—you were either going up a hill or down one. She hiked up a half mile to a bus stop and sat down. The stop was never used anymore and the bus that once ran this line was as dead as the woman in the parked car below. Vitoria saw it from her vantage point. Time to erase her tracks. If she wanted this to be a career, she'd have to be careful. She took out her phone, punched in a code, and made a call.

The car exploded. The back end lifted off the ground, throwing the car forward. Shattered glass hit the pavement and flames burst out. The police would find it and the woman—well, what was left of her—and make the connection to the Blondes.

The Blondes were not just micro-kidnappers anymore—they were moving up the food chain. And if Vitoria had anything to do with it, they would make history. She'd be one of the first filthy-rich women to actually earn money herself, without the help of any man.

Man or woman—she didn't care who she killed to get to the top.

# CHAPTER 6

MANDY PACED THE ROOM as I pulled a baby-blue sundress over my head. "Gah. Where is my dragon bracelet?"

We were getting ready to go out to a lobster dinner at a restaurant downtown. The concierge said it was the best lobster in Rio.

"The one Rick got you for your anniversary?"

"Yeah. I was wearing it when we flew in, but now it's gone."

I was about to make a snarky comment when I noticed how upset she was. That bracelet had been given to her on their fifth anniversary, and Mandy was very sentimental about gifts. I think she still had the Backstreet Boys poster I'd given her for her fourteenth birthday. So I got on my hands and knees and hunted under the bed and chairs for it, but no luck.

"Do you think it was stolen?" she said, her eyebrows creased in worry.

"Not likely. It probably slipped off your wrist."

But she wasn't listening. "I bet I know who stole it." Her eyes went wide. "That bellhop girl."

"Whoa, whoa, honey. You're pointing fingers awful fast."

She continued pacing. "I bet she's in an abusive situation and is saving up to get out of here. That little thief. I even gave her an extra twenty dollars."

"What are you gonna do? Search her locker?"

She stopped in her tracks. "You think I should?"

"No," I exclaimed, laughing. "I think you should calm down and look through your suitcase and purse again. You're always losing things and then finding them ten minutes later."

As she riffled through her purse, she muttered, "This is it. This is the mystery I have to solve. I have to figure out where it is."

I chimed in. "It's 'The Girl with the Missing Dragon Tattoo Bracelet.'" I pulled my hair back into a messy bun and chose simple silver hoop earrings to accent my dress.

Mandy wore a slip and still had her hair up in a towel. "We should report it. I bet there are cameras in the halls—we could get them to show us the last few hours and see who was in our room."

"Mandy, come on—I'm sure it will turn up. I don't think anyone stole it."

"Sarah Steele, this is our first case in Rio. The bellhop might be a part of a gang, and she took it to draw us out. Then, when we find her, she'll drug us and sell us on the black market as sex slaves." Mandy turned toward the bathroom, but not before I saw the smile she was hiding.

"Then we'd best not risk it," I said. "Rest in peace, dragon bracelet."

"Sure, fine, whatever," she called from the other room. "You handle important cases for work all the time, but you can't help your best friend out."

"Tell you what. If we can't find it by tomorrow, I'll go to the front desk and demand to see the surveillance tapes. We'll get to the bottom of this dragon bracelet thing, okay?"

"Fine, but I'm not kidding—it was stolen."

When I heard the blow dryer start, I peeked in the bathroom. She was drying her hair and painting her toenails at the same time.

"How long's this gonna take?"

She sent me a sharp look. "You can't rush perfection."

"Well then, Mary Poppins, I'm going on a walk. Meet you outside on the patio. Try to be done before Christmas."

As I left the room, the Blondes came to mind. Solomon had texted not to go anywhere alone. Shrugging, I softly closed the door. I wouldn't leave sight of the hotel. What were the odds that I'd get kidnapped on my way to the beach? Even with my penchant for trouble, no one was that unlucky. Besides, if the Blondes took me for my money, they'd be the unlucky ones. My savings account could only buy a couple pairs of Jimmy Choos.

# CHAPTER 5

VITORIA'S HEART STILL HADN'T slowed by the time Mia, her first-in-command, picked her up. She swerved to a stop in front of her. The white Jeep was an older '02 model. They traded in cars after every job. Emilia knew a guy who got them a great deal.

Mia knew where to go. They'd talked over this plan for a month, ever since their contact had made the first call. Mia was a good driver. She knew when to gun it and what alleys to take. She used the horn superfluously, cursing out the window as if the other drivers had ridiculed her mother.

They got to the hotel and everything slowed. That's just the way the tourists liked it: slow. People meandered along the walk. They lazily talked in the shade, strolled to the beach, and drank martinis in lounge chairs—it was enough to make Vitoria's blood boil. These people had never worked an honest day in their lives. They deserved to be robbed. She wanted their money to go to people who had calluses on their hands ... after she collected a hefty percentage for herself, of course.

The sun lost its zenith, fading in the sky. Vitoria calmed, her blood no longer pumped full of adrenaline. She missed it. Some people loved the thrill and escape of drugs or alcohol or extreme sports—she needed this. She couldn't wait for the next bit of excitement, the feeling of losing all control.

"They should be looking for her by now," Mia said.

Vitoria just nodded. An odd peace settled over her. There was no unease in her soul from what she'd done—it settled just right. The woman had deserved it and no one would even miss her.

"Hey, look," Mia whispered.

Their target walked out of the hotel. She was prettier than her picture and wore stilettos with a short dress. If she were poor, people would say she dressed like a hooker, but because she was rich, they called her stylish.

"Put on your mask." Vitoria pulled a thin black ski mask from her pocket and pulled it over her head. She adjusted the air conditioning so it blasted in her face. Despite that, sweat trickled down her cheek.

"Let's roll."

# CHAPTER 6

I MADE MY WAY down to the lobby and caught several passing looks from men and women both as I walked out the front door. I was not used to such attention. Most the time I was in business attire and wore a shark-type attitude. But here, I felt different—relaxed. It felt good to be dressed down, I smiled easily, and I felt like I didn't have to be on my guard.

After taking a step outside, I had to close my eyes and pause, enjoying the breeze. It ruffled my hair playfully and smelled like flowers and sea salt.

Chills suddenly went up my arms and I knew someone was watching me. I opened my eyes to see the valet sitting on a stool in front of his podium, wearing a cheeky grin.

He had white, shoulder-length dreadlocks with beads and feathers in them, and his face was covered in freckles. He bowed slightly. "Need a car?"

"No, thanks. Just going for a walk." Even though his grin was on the lewd side, his eyes looked light, as if he meant no harm. With a nod, I started walking.

"Sure thing," he said. "Be careful out there. Them Blondes love your type."

I stopped short. What did he know about them? "Blondes?"

He looked down and tugged on his dark red vest. "Yes, the Blondes. You've heard of 'em, haven't you? They kidnap wealthy women tourists and take their money. Credit cards and the like. Max the cards out in a few hours and let their captives go afterwards. It's been going on for some time now and the authorities can't catch 'em."

"I wouldn't be a target—I'm not exactly loaded with bullion."

He squinted at me. "They all blonde, that's why they call 'em the Blondes. Though none of 'em have been identified. You look like one of 'em—maybe you *is* one of 'em." He chuckled as if it were a hilarious joke.

"If I were, you wouldn't know it anyway, would you..." I checked out his nametag. "Marco?"

Marco laughed nervously. "No, I guess not."

"But they don't hurt anyone?"

"No way. Never. They're just after the cash." He lowered his voice. "Did you know they give money to orphanages and families and churches that need it?"

That was interesting. "So they're like Zorro? Taking from the rich and giving to the poor?" Something about that struck a chord in me and I spoke without thinking. "More power to them."

Marco's eyes rose in surprise, and then he settled on his chair with a grunt. "Amen. But you be careful."

"I will." They could probably recognize that my shoes didn't cost more than thirty bucks and thus I wouldn't be worth their trouble. Plus, I figured I could take them. In fact, it might be kind of fun to pit myself against a gang of girls.

Wait, that was stupid. I was here to relax. Relax, and eat lobster. I made my way toward the beach.

The heat and humidity were heavy, but in a weird way, I loved it.

The weather was a presence—it had weight.

A warm breeze came off the ocean. I walked down a concrete path that reminded me of the Greenbelt back home. People jogged, rode bikes, and walked. There were a few hundred yards of sand between the path and the water. It was scattered with seashells. I was half tempted to scrap dinner and go sit on the beach again to watch the sun go down. Maybe we would have time to do that after dinner.

Squealing car tires rent the air. The hair on the back of my neck stood up straight. A white Jeep sped across the American hotel parking lot and flew out the exit. It narrowly missed hitting a car, which swerved and honked. Why were they in such a hurry?

There was a figure on the concrete lying on his back. I rushed over, my heels clicking on the pavement.

As I neared, I heard him calling, "Help, please, help. Someone. Policia—"

"Sir, are you okay?" I ran up to him as fast as my heels would allow. He had a terrible gash on his forehead and his eyes were glazed, as if in shock.

"Tanya. Tanya … they took Tanya." Jerking quickly to his feet, he wobbled like a drunk man and would've fallen on his face if I hadn't put my shoulder under his arm and held him steady.

"Sir, you should sit," I said in a soothing tone, lowering him to the concrete before he crushed me. A couple approached, eyes wide, and I asked them to go tell the hotel manager and call the police.

The man put his head between his knees. Blood trickled down his cheek from the wound on his forehead. Judging from his worn skin and the white hair above his ears, he was probably in his late forties. He wore a slim-fitting T-shirt, designer jeans, and shoes that looked like they cost more than my whole shoe collection. But his watch stood out—it was a cheap plastic piece with a cracked face. I let go of him, but he didn't release my arm.

"They took her." He looked over at me, eyes scared. "They took Tanya."

"Who took her?" I asked, although I had a feeling I knew the answer before he even said it.

"Girls in ski masks." He took a quivering breath.

Had it been the Blondes? A morbid thrill went up my spine. They'd been so close to me.

"What happened?"

His speech was choppy as he tried to sort through his thoughts. "Two girls. Both blonde. Sped up to me and Tanya. One came at me fast. Punched me so hard, I fell down. Then they shoved Tanya in the car. Her face. She was so scared. She didn't even scream."

His eyes cleared, and he looked at me as if for the first time. Then his expression shadowed. "If they hurt her, I'll kill them." The panic choked his voice.

My heart melted to see him so upset. He looked like a man who was strong and in control—even the way he spoke at this moment was sure—but he was breaking down.

"Shh, I know." I took a Kleenex from my purse and dabbed it on his forehead to stem the bleeding, which had slowed already. "From what you've told me, they might be a gang called the Blondes. They're micro-kidnappers."

"What's that?"

"It's when they kidnap the victim for a couple of hours, max out all their credit cards, and then drop them off in another part of town."

He clenched his jaw, and his hands shook.

"Unharmed," I finished.

"Oh, thank God." He swallowed, wincing as I pressed the Kleenex to his gash. I was surprised the hotel managers weren't out here already. Perhaps they were too busy calling their lawyers.

"Now you should go inside to wait for the police and get your wound cleaned up."

He took my hand and sucked in a shuddering breath. He was on the verge of tears. "She must be so scared—she doesn't handle stress very well. I should never have … She said this vacation was a bad idea …" He trailed off. I gave him time to recover. I remembered when I was in a similar situation and the feeling of possibly losing a loved one flooded back, making my gut hurt.

"Sir, we should get you inside. And you should report this immediately. Your brain loses details of the memory every second you don't write it down."

"The Jeep didn't have a license plate," he said quickly. "I noticed that."

"Was there anything particular about the girls?"

"They were young, I think. I didn't see their faces. Their clothes were simple—T-shirts and jeans. I didn't notice anything else. Except …"

"What?"

"There was a mini surfboard attached to their rearview mirror."

"That's a good detail—anything like that will help the police find them. Though they'll probably ditch the car soon enough."

"My wife and I are staying in the Palms Hotel, right there." He pointed to the very expensive-looking hotel on the other side of the parking lot. "We were going to look for her friend who never came back from her shopping trip this afternoon. Do you think they took her too?" The more we talked, the steadier he became. He took the Kleenex from me, and after pressing it to his forehead another second, threw the blood-soaked tissue on the pavement.

This case was getting more interesting by the second. "That's worth telling the police. What's your friend's name?"

"Nancy Parker." He looked closer at me. "Who are you?"

"My name is Sarah Steele. I'm an assistant district attorney back home in the States. Just taking a vacation. Who are you?" I helped him up.

"Eddie Lofton, state representative of Nebraska. We're on vacation as well, our twentieth anniversary. It was my gift to her."

My BS sensor went off at that. If the Loftons were on an anniversary vacation, why would she bring a friend? That could mean their marriage was ... I stopped myself. I told my brain to stop trying to solve the case and just help the guy.

Eddie cleared his throat. "So we have a lead already, these ... Blondes."

"Can't say for sure. From your description, I'd say they fit the bill, but I don't know very much. You really should talk to the police."

We went slowly across the parking lot toward the lobby. I still had my arm looped through his to steady him. But as we walked he stood up straighter, took a deep breath, and seemed to find his strength. When he looked down at me, I saw the panic was gone and determination was in its place. "I should call the credit card companies and cancel them."

I shook my head. "You should wait for the police and see what they say first. You don't want to piss off the gang if they're trying to use her cards."

The hotel manager and security came running out of the hotel with harried expressions.

Before they reached us, Eddie turned to me with a grave face. "It seems extra beneficial to have a lawyer at my side. Will you come with me to the police station and embassy to get this worked out?" His voice was professional, but his eyes pled with me.

I bit my lip. On the one hand, here was a man in need asking for help. On the other, I felt like it was something the police could handle, and he didn't really need me to babysit him. Then I caught sight of a figure walking across the parking lot, looking worried. Mandy. Her face was full of distrust, as if I had sought out this bit of trouble.

The sea wind blew gently and the gulls called above. I inhaled and smelled diesel, but beyond that was the unmistakable scent of budding flowers. It pulled me out of myself, out of crisis mode, and helped me see the bigger picture.

There had to be a point where I could just walk away and not try to save the world. Other people could take care of this—it was their job.

The manager and security reached us and instantly started asking twenty questions, but Eddie didn't take his eyes off me. I slowly shook my head, looking at Mandy. "I really think the police and embassy will help you more than I can."

His shoulders slumped a bit and I felt a pang of guilt for not helping him. I slipped my card out of my purse and handed it to him. Mandy shot me a disapproving look. "But if things don't go smoothly, give me a call and I'll come right away." I heard sirens wailing in the distance.

Eddie shook my hand, gripping it like he wouldn't let go. "Just come with me to the station."

"I'm sorry, no. I hope your wife is found quickly." I gave him a small smile.

That's when security pulled him away. He entered the building with a backwards glance in my direction.

I mentally said goodbye to him, and to the case. The only mystery I wanted to solve here in Rio was Mandy's missing bracelet.

She came up beside me with an eyebrow cocked. "You spend five hours in Rio and already you—"

"Refused to help a state representative find his kidnapped wife."

Mandy gasped. "Geez."

"Two blonde girls took her. The police can handle it." I started toward our hotel, where a cab waited in front of Marco's podium. Mandy must have ordered it for us.

"We'll be much too busy parasailing and surfing and getting our nails done to work on that."

She was right. There was a time for everything. A time to get involved and a time to stand back. A time to work and a time to eat huge lobster dinners.

"Ready for the best lobster you'll ever eat in your life? They're so fresh they'll be crawling off your plate." Mandy climbed into the cab.

"Where's my bib?"

As I closed the cab door, I hoped whoever got Eddie's case was good at his job. His vulnerability and fear still haunted me, and I didn't want to imagine what Tanya was going through. Promising myself to check on him later, I did my best to put it out of my mind.

# CHAPTER 8

VITORIA LOOKED PAST HER new patent leather boots, propped up on her desk, to the three women who were bragging about their latest plunder. They all had long blonde hair. Handbags were piled on the wooden table stretched along the east wall. Emilia giggled and pranced around the room in a long fur coat. It was at least a hundred and ten degrees in the warehouse they called their "cave," and yet she pranced. They'd searched for an abandoned building with fast exits in every direction and had found this. Their little headquarters wasn't much more than a barn—a wooden structure, square and open, filled with trunks and wooden shipping crates. There were two new Ducatis parked in one corner. A desk and a makeshift office sat in the other corner, which was Vitoria's domain.

It wasn't glamorous, but it was safe.

Tied to a chair with duct tape was the rich white woman. She'd stopped struggling ten minutes ago.

"The thing I love about this is the shoes. God, I could have a thousand pairs and it still wouldn't be enough," Lili said. "Platforms, stilettos, sandals, boots, Choo, Vuitton, Miu Miu, Gucci—gimme, gimme, gimme." She giggled. She was the shortest one of the gang, and the youngest. And acted like it.

"You can have the shoes. Give me the clothes." Emilia sighed and tossed the fur coat into a cardboard mailing box. "I don't think I could go back to normal clothes ever again. But lucky for me I don't have to dress down." She laughed at that and kicked off her heels, glancing at the captive woman. Vitoria watched the exchange between Emilia and the rich brat. Emilia's eyes held more compassion than she liked to see. She had weird principles, that one.

They were taking their sweet time. Lili should have been off making payments already. When they paid key people in the *favela*, they earned loyalty. A deep, abiding loyalty. Vitoria knew almost everyone in the *favela* would take a bullet for the Blondes. It was a heady power.

Mia was the quiet one, and the only one acting like a responsible adult at the moment. She was black, with dyed blonde hair, tall and lithe and strong. They'd known each other since they were teens. She tagged and cataloged the shoes, and packed them into a box according to brand and size. They would go into a crate and get shipped to one of their buyers to be sold online just under the store cost. It was quite a lucrative business.

"Lili, Emilia, come here." Vitoria had to get the two wild cards back in order, and prepare them for what was to come. Lili bowed slightly and Emilia plopped herself on the leather couch to the side of the desk.

"Comfortable?" Vitoria swung her legs off the desk and stood.

"Very. I'm so glad we got air conditioning in here, but it's still hot." Emilia's whiny voice grated on Vitoria.

"I don't care if you're hot, and I don't care if you like shoes or fur coats. What I do care about is the royal mess you created out there today," she yelled. The two girls dropped their smiles and looked down at the floor.

"Look at me." Their heads snapped up. "This is not a game. Do I need to remind you what you had before? Nothing. That's right. Nothing. And now you live like that rich American slut sitting over there." She pointed at Tanya Lofton. "Emilia, when you watched her after we got back, you were supposed to keep your mouth shut, but you talked, didn't you?"

Emilia looked over at Lili and then back at Vitoria. "Yes."

"You don't talk to the marks."

"Yes, but I was just letting her know that it won't be long—"

"Don't."

Lili wisely kept silent, and Emilia bit her lower lip. She opened her mouth to say something, but decided against it.

"And you, Lili." Lili flinched and swallowed hard. "You can't just buy what you want. You have a list. But what did you do?"

Lili shifted her weight from one foot to the other. "I went back to the same store."

"And what do we *never* do?"

"We never shop at the same store twice."

"That's right. We never shop at the same store twice. We can shop for a year and never walk into the same store twice, but you just had to go back, didn't you?"

Vitoria paced in front of her desk and tried to calm down. She had to get them to fear her. Not just fear her, but respect her leadership. Up until now, they all thought this was some high school game, like the cons they used to pull on tourists. But this was not just a con. The game was a lot bigger now.

Mia tossed her hair and kept on working. At least one of them got it.

Tanya started struggling. She got one hand free and tugged on her restraints. One of her arms got loose. Vitoria cursed and rushed over, pulling out her .45.

"Going somewhere?"

Tanya Lofton took off her blindfold just as Vitoria backhanded her with the butt of the gun. Blood gushed from her mouth and she toppled over, crashing to the floor. Crying out, she fought to get free, but her tied arm was pinned under the chair, most likely broken. Now the rich woman knew what it felt like to be broke.

Emilia called out something, but Vitoria was not paying attention. Tanya was crying and blood ran down her cheek where a deep gash had opened up.

Vitoria grabbed her by the shoulders and righted her chair. She shoved the gun into Tanya's mouth. Her teeth clattered against the metal and she froze. The room fell silent and even Mia stopped what she was doing.

"Shh, *querida*," Vitoria whispered.

Tears made tracks on Tanya's blood-streaked cheeks.

"That's right, just relax. I need you to do something for me, something only you can do …" Pulling the trigger, she blew out the back of Tanya's head.

# CHAPTER 3

TWO GLASSES OF RED wine later, I was feeling much better. The lobster was divine. It had been steamed and the tail grilled, and we dipped it in herb butter. The flesh was succulent and bursting with flavor. We ordered chocolate covered strawberries for dessert, and Mandy talked about the plans she and Rick had for remodeling their house.

The restaurant had an open patio with a view of the sea. I half-listened to her as I watched the sun set over the horizon. Orange and pink saturated the sky. It was perfect.

"So, you up for a little fun tonight?" Mandy draped her arm over the back of her chair.

I pretended to be uninterested. "Would this fun involve a slimy dance club and sweaty guys trying to hit on us all night?"

"I sure hope so. I mean, it's on my list. Rick said to be good, but not a nun. That means I can flirt a little, maybe even let some hot Rio guy dance me up." Her eyes sparkled and her bright pink dress almost glowed in the dim balcony lighting.

"Hmm. Well, I guess we could see what we see." Knowing Mandy, she'd already booked our reservations.

"Oh, good. I Googled some clubs and I found one that looks a-maz-ing."

"Figured as much. Okay, let's stay up all night and then I just might be able to sleep in."

I checked my phone again and resisted texting Solomon. He'd been silent, more than I was used to.

"Really? You're going twitterpated on me in the middle of a conversation?"

I slid my phone back into my purse. "What?"

"You know what. You and that dumb look on your face—it's like watching a bunny hump a balloon."

I about choked on my drink. "Mandy, you're killing me." I laughed so hard that the group at the next table turned to stare at us.

After I could breathe again, I flicked a piece of bread at Mandy. "You can't do that to me when I'm drinking. You know I had a bunny when I was a kid, and he …" I started to laugh again.

Mandy wiped bread crumbs off her dress and smiled. "I know all about your bunny and his balloons. It was just wrong. But I gotta say, he was a gentle lover—never once popped one."

Good thing I hadn't taken another drink or else I would've spit it out my nose.

# CHAPTER 10

THE DANCE CLUB WAS in a remodeled factory in what I considered the sleazy part of town. The main door was on the second floor and as soon as the bouncer let us in, we had to wait in line on some creepy metal stairs for almost an hour. I was getting pissed. Just when I was about to call it a night and drag Mandy back to the hotel, the line moved.

When I walked through the second set of doors leading into the main part of the club, everything changed. Music pulsed through my body and, despite myself, I couldn't stop moving to the beat.

Mandy yelled over the music. "I hear this is the hottest club in Rio—three floors, balcony catwalks, and even a rooftop bar."

"Sounds great."

"What?" The music was crazy loud—we were getting closer to the main floor.

I yelled in Mandy's ear, "Just keep close to me. I'm not looking for you if you run off."

"Okay," she yelled back.

At the bottom of the staircase, the room opened up and I was amazed by the size of the place. A huge open area moved with dancing bodies like a sea of hands and arms. Laser lights rotated around the room, and beyond the dance floor was a main stage with a full band. There was a lead singer, two drummers, and a woman with a bright blue Mohawk who played an electric guitar. Fog spilled from around the stage. I grinned like an idiot.

"Sweet. Look, they have a bar up there too." Mandy pointed to a balcony area where more people danced. The building was old, with rusted metal beams, exposed wires, and duct work covering the high ceiling.

"I think the place is about to fall down. What do you think?"

"You need a drink? Yeah, me too." Mandy worked her way through the crowd and leaned against the bar. It, unlike the building, was new and modern. Made of glass that glowed blue, it almost looked like it was hovering above the floor.

Mandy ordered some shots of something green. I shook my head and tossed back my drink. Ugh. Tasted like mouthwash.

"There you go, Sarah. Now you're loosening up." Mandy smiled and handed me another shot. This one was pink.

"To our vacation."

"To a fun, *relaxing* vacation," Mandy said. "And getting everything checked off my list."

We clinked glasses. I liked this shot better—it tasted like cotton candy. Mandy grabbed my hand and pulled me toward the dance floor. We mixed in with the crowd and I couldn't help but move with the beat. One guy sidled up to me. He had spiked hair and wore a purple polo with a popped collar. Judging by the way his eyes still hadn't reached my face, I labeled him a cad. I turned my back to him and scanned the room. When at clubs, I didn't look for guys who were hot—I searched for guys who were good dancers. After all, I wasn't here to find a boyfriend. I was here to dance. I finally spotted one guy with brilliant rhythm, made eye contact with him, and then for the next hour we had fun swinging and moving and dancing. He was talented enough to make me look good as long as I followed his lead, and I learned a lot of new moves.

There were a hundred people on the floor, maybe more, and I got warm. Which is lady-speak for sweating like a pig. After giving my partner a kiss on the cheek and a wave goodbye, I grabbed Mandy.

"Let's go up to the rooftop bar and get some fresh air," I yelled. Tossing her hair back, she nodded.

Some guy groped me as I pulled Mandy through the dancers. I slapped his hand away and pointed a stern finger at his face. He just laughed and moved on.

Metal stairs and ladders ran everywhere. I wasn't sure which one led to the roof, so I headed for the closest one. I tripped on the way up and hit my knee—hard. I gritted my teeth and Mandy laughed behind me. "You haven't even had three drinks yet."

"Shut it." I muttered a curse and looked at my knee. No blood.

The second floor was not as large, but it was cool. Neon couches and high tables lined the back wall and the bar was in the middle. The balcony overlooked the floor below and was just as packed as the rest of the place.

"Nice. At least I don't have to yell up here. Hey, I bet that's the roof." Mandy pointed to another set of stairs.

"Let's go up. If I don't get some air, I may pass out." I was glad I had worn a light dress.

We headed up the stairs. At the top, a heavy guy in a dark blue suit held up his hand. He smiled and motioned to a sign.

*VIP Floor*, written in English and three other languages.

"Oh, come on. We came all the way here from Boise, Idaho, and you won't let us in?" Mandy put her hands on her hips, but the bouncer shook his head. Two girls wearing matching black leather outfits ducked past us and the fat guy let them through.

"Great. Now what?" I was annoyed, to say the least.

A good-looking man with mellow eyes came up behind us. Mandy looked him up and down, and then smiled. He smiled back, said something in Portuguese to the bouncer, and touched the back of my arm. I had studied a little Portuguese before the trip, but I had no clue what he'd said.

"Well, hello, Mr. Knight in Shining Armor." Mandy curled her finger through her hair and tilted her head. I held back a groan.

"Hello, ladies. I'm Rafa." He had a thick accent. "We go."

The bouncer smiled and stepped aside.

Rafa took us, one on each arm, and led us up the stairs into the night air. We were so high that I saw a few stars shining through the city haze. The wind, although still hot, felt good. Rafa was not as tall as I was, but very nice-looking. He had an old-fashioned air about him. Must be the mustache and twenties-style suit.

"Rafa, do you live around here?" Mandy spun around to face him and he smiled.

"Ladies, please drink." Rafa flicked his finger and waiters and drinks appeared like magic. From the looks we were getting, I pegged him as someone very well known, but I feared his English was limited to "hello," "ladies," and "drink." He liked to stick to the basics.

"Great," I said. "We're getting hit on by a guy who can only say 'hello.'"

Rafa grinned again and said, "Hello." He held up his glass and we toasted to nothing.

Mandy laughed. "I bet he can say 'yes.' All men can say 'yes,' no matter the language barrier."

"Yes." Rafa slipped his hand to my lower back and skillfully pulled me to the dance floor. Dang, he was good.

The rooftop bar made the space below look rundown. There was a long table full of appetizers and desserts. The drinks up here were on the house. I wondered who was footing the bill.

"Rafa, do you understand what I'm saying and just can't speak English well, or do you not get a word of it?"

He smiled and kissed my cheek. "Yes." He pointed at his chest and said, "Rafa."

I tried to remember some of the Portuguese I studied, but most of it was how to ask for the bathroom or how much the clothes were or when to get off the bus.

I wanted him to know I was having a good time and thank him for letting us upstairs, so I said something I thought meant that I liked it up here.

His eyes lit up and he licked his lips. He pulled me in closer so my chest was pressed against his. My heart sped up. I liked my personal space, and this was way out of my comfort zone.

"Hey, can I cut in?" Mandy yanked me to her and Rafa stepped back. After a frown of annoyance, he bowed slightly and walked to the bar. In a minute he was chatting up a tall blonde in killer heels.

"Thanks, friend."

"Yo, what did you tell him? He was all over you."

"I said I liked it up here … I think." I grabbed my phone and spoke into my translator app. My phone translated it, and I read the screen and groaned. I turned it toward Mandy and she laughed.

"You'd like his clothes off. Ha! He probably thinks he hit the jackpot."

I glanced over and looked away quickly. "Great, he's staring at us. Let's get out of here."

Mandy snorted. "Why? He is hot and rich, and you're single, unlike me."

"I'm not available. I'm dating Solomon."

"You won't even call him your boyfriend."

"Well, I'm not making out with some drug lord named Rafa. He's good-looking, yes, but kind of creepy." I danced us toward the edge of the building and looked out over Rio.

The city was pretty with all its twinkling lights, but it had a dark gloom hanging over it. Or was it just me?

"Wow, what a view." Mandy leaned on the railing and sighed. "Even the slums look good at night, with all the lights and laughter. And look at that moon."

"Yeah, not a bad view for a couple of Boise girls."

Mandy side-hugged me and we watched the full moon hang there. I could smell the ocean and it made me sleepy. I was partied out, though it wasn't even past two in the morning.

"You about ready to call it a nigh—" My phone vibrated and I yanked it from my purse, relieved that Solomon wasn't MIA anymore. But the text wasn't from Solomon.

*Miss Steele, they found Tanya. Please come.*

It was Eddie Lofton.

# CHAPTER 11

EDDIE LOFTON SAT IN a stiff couch in his hotel lobby. His eyes were bloodshot. Mandy pulled up a chair from a nearby table. I paced in front of them, too jittery to sit.

Muscular men in suits stood not far behind Eddie. Their eyes moved around the room, but they stayed as still as statues.

Eddie's voice was rough. "I'm sorry for contacting you so late, but I just didn't know what to do. I don't know anyone here, and—"

"I'm glad you did. What happened? Is your wife …?" I didn't want to say the word, but by the look on his face, I knew. She was dead.

"They found her body in the slums, in a Dumpster." His voice broke, but he managed to hold it together. "They shot her in the head."

Mandy gasped and muttered, "Oh my God."

My mind whirled. Maybe it wasn't the Blondes after all—they never killed their victims. Tanya must've been targeted because of her husband—why would they kill her over a few credit cards? Or perhaps something had gone wrong with the Blondes.

"Are there any leads?" I didn't want to push him, but the whole thing made my head buzz.

Eddie ran his hand through his salt-and-pepper hair and nodded.

"They believe it was that gang, the Blondes. They found a note shoved in her mouth." A spark lit his eye—he was angry. "It said, 'All rich belong in the ditch.'"

Mandy put a comforting hand on his arm. "I'm so sorry, Mr. Lofton."

He kept on talking, as if he was in a trance. "They found Nancy too. Her body was in a bombed-out car in an abandoned parking lot. The Jeep from yesterday was found under a bridge, burned out. No DNA evidence was recovered. The police don't have any leads." His shoulders slumped.

Lady Justice was out of her league here. From the little I knew from reading about them, it would take superheroes to bring the Blondes in. They could hide from the law for years in any of the shacks lining the mountains. The Blondes were heroes on the other side of the tracks, so no one would give any information on them. They would also have enough resources to split the country at any moment.

What bothered me most was why the Blondes had suddenly changed. Why go from a successful Robin Hood micro-kidnapping venture to murdering a high-profile person? It wasn't just dumb coincidence that they killed both Tanya and Nancy—someone had picked them on purpose. Or Eddie. I eyed him with renewed interest.

Eddie's eyes weren't just cloudy with grief—they were hopeless. "Why would someone do this to us?"

"God," Mandy said again. Her eyes watered. We exchanged a look, and I was touched by her compassion. I raised my eyebrows, creasing them in question. We communicated via expression, which we had perfected during high school classes, and she finished the silent conversation with a subtle nod of her head.

That was it. We'd take the case. Sleeping in would just have to wait until the Blondes were behind bars.

# CHAPTER 12

A PLAN SIMMERED IN my mind.

I put a hand on Eddie's shoulder. He still hadn't taken a sip of water. "Eddie, have you eaten today?"

He shook his head.

"Can you?"

He was about to shake his head again when he paused. "I guess I could. But—" He glanced toward the restaurant.

"You don't want to be around people?" I guessed.

He nodded.

Mandy stood up, as if doing something would ease the tension. "I'll order for you from the restaurant and bring it up when it's done. What do you want?" She pulled out her phone and took his order— chicken tenders with fries and ranch on the side. I ordered a steak salad, and I knew Mandy would get her usual grilled chicken Caesar salad.

"Why don't we go back to your room?" I suggested. More clues about him and Tanya would be there, and he'd probably be more comfortable answering our questions.

Eddie led me up to the third floor, and I texted Mandy the room number. I don't know what I was expecting, but a simple queen bed and room without-a-view wasn't it. His suitcase was open in the corner and neat rolls of clothes and accessories were piled in it. No sign of a woman's suitcase—until I noticed an adjoining door leading to the next room, unlocked and cracked open. So they weren't even sharing bedrooms. Didn't sound like the romantic getaway most couples go on for their anniversary—more like eighth-grade camp.

His laptop was propped up on the desk, which had a fake leather top and an ugly green lamp peering over it. That was my target.

Eddie sat heavily on the bed and rubbed the bristles on his chin. He looked like he would either fall asleep or lose a gasket any second—anger and hurt were written all over him. "What can we do to get those bitches?"

That was the kind of determination I liked to hear. I could work with it. "Have you checked to see where they used the credit cards?"

He went and sat at the desk, leaning over his keyboard. I took out my phone. Pretending to be consumed with my screen, I glanced over his shoulder as he typed in his username and password. Using some association techniques I'd learned from a book on retention, I logged it away to retrieve later. After getting to the bank's website, he glanced suspiciously at me, and when he saw I was engaged with my phone, typed in his information. I mentally rolled my eyes at his password: OMAHA71baseball. I could have hacked that on my own.

Strolling to the chair, I sat down and finished my text to Solomon. *Beach. Lobster. Dancing. Drinking. Rio agrees with me so far.* I left out the part about being entangled in the very thing he'd asked me to avoid—the Blondes. What he didn't know wouldn't hurt him.

Thinking of him made me think of the FBI. "Are the feds coming from the U.S.?"

"Yes." Eddie looked up from the screen. "They'll be here tomorrow."

That'd be another chance for me to back out—with the feds on the

Blondes' trail, perhaps I could go back to vacation mode. That is, once I knew someone I trusted was on the case.

"See here." Eddie pointed at the screen. "They maxed out our two credit cards at …" he counted. "Seven different stores. That's ten thousand."

I gave a low whistle. That wasn't petty cash. Looked like the stores were all department stores, except one that could be a car dealer. Later, I'd get back in his account and snoop further. For now, I tried to put together an idea of what turned them from thieves to murderers.

I went through the scenarios in my mind. "Did Nancy or Tanya know self-defense?"

Eddie stared blankly at me.

"If Nancy had escalated the situation, fought back, or seen their faces, they'd have to kill her."

Eddie objected. "A car bomb is an elaborate way to deal with a feisty victim. But no, Nancy couldn't have taken anyone down. She was about thirty pounds overweight and had bad knees. And Tanya." He scoffed. "She couldn't even defend herself from a spider. She'd scream at me to kill them anytime she saw one."

I raised my eyebrows. "Well, spiders are quite terrifying."

"Quite. But all that to say that she couldn't throw a punch to save her life." He let out a tight laugh. "And she was big on gun control, too—wouldn't let me buy a gun or even pick one up. Said it'd be bad for my image." He rubbed his knuckles, and then turned back to the screen.

So it sounded like Tanya enjoyed telling Eddie what to do, and he didn't like it. But I was still only seeing things from his perspective. Although he looked like a respectable man, I knew there were two sides to every story. Details. I needed details. With my phone, I sent a quick email to my intern, Joshua, back at the office, asking him to get me a list of Eddie and Tanya's enemies and also any dirt on Eddie he could find. Joshua, who was a wide-eyed, sheltered Hawaiian native, was incredibly gifted at finding dirt on people. I was sure he'd get back to me with something.

Leaning back in the chair, I watched Eddie as he scrolled through news sites. Tanya's picture was everywhere. There were probably a dozen news teams headed to Rio to get the story—now to get his side of it. I started my interrogation.

My first rule: Never ask a straight question. My second rule: Let them underestimate you. Third rule: Make rabbit trails. Sometimes the clue that broke the case came from a random detail.

"What's with the watch?" I stared at the cheap, scratched plastic watch he wore.

Eddie shut the lid of the laptop and turned to me, running his hand through his hair. His eyes were heavy-lidded and sleepy. "It's to remind me where I came from. Before I ran for mayor, when I was barely making ends meet as a carpenter, I splurged on this forty-dollar watch from Walmart. Now I wear it every day to remind me of the value of forty dollars."

The words deepened my respect for him. "I think I remember reading about your race in the papers. What was your slogan—'We can fix it'? Or you were called the carpenter or something?"

He grinned. It made him seem so much younger, and roguish. "Yeah, I was the carpenter."

I raised my eyebrows "The media went wild with your hard-working, honest American character. They said you couldn't be bought out by any corporations. Your campaign was funded by more civilian dollars than any other campaign in history. You won by a landslide, didn't you?"

His eyes glinted in memory. "It seems so long ago."

"But you're still the hard-working, honest American carpenter." I phrased it so it could be a statement or a question.

He slowly nodded. "I'm just building something more complicated than tables."

"Bet you wish you could just work on tables some days."

"Yeah." His shoulders slumped. The burden of his civil service weighed heavily on him.

"Do you still refuse to take money from corporations?"

"That's my policy."

"Hmm." Was he telling the truth? Not taking corporate money would be nearly impossible in this political climate. I knew how D.C. worked—he couldn't accomplish anything if he didn't have a company or two that owed him a favor. That was something else I'd have to check out.

"Did Tanya have any personal enemies?"

An unmistakable look of guilt crossed his features. "Yes. Me."

I looked down, pretending not to be shocked at his admission.

He continued. "Tanya worked for GenEarth, an environmental company that tries to keep the earth the way it was before the industrial revolution." He rolled his eyes. "I think she would've been happier if everyone drove buggies and washed their clothes by hand—that is, as long as she had servants to do her share of the work. GenEarth was suing the State, two energy companies, five waste-disposal companies, and three water plants. She wanted them shut down." He sighed heavily. "Tanya was the face for their law department as well, so she's the one people targeted. She got hate mail every day and not a few threatening phone calls. It wasn't just the stuff she said that got people riled up against her—it was the way she said it. I … I … I really, um, disliked her for it." He cleared his throat. "But I wanted things to get better between us, so I booked this trip. It was our last chance."

He spoke in short bursts, as if he was nervous, but I had to keep him talking. "Have you heard of the Blondes before?"

"Not until I read about them in the paper after booking the trip."

"And this is your first time to Rio?"

"Yes."

"Did she have life insurance?"

"No. Neither do I. We have a savings account with enough money to last us if either one of us died."

"Does she have family?"

"She has five sisters and a brother. They will be … so devastated. She was always the ringleader at holidays and came up with new traditions. Last year at Thanksgiving, we had a hot dog roast instead of a turkey. I can't imagine the family without her."

My shoulders wilted. Things weren't smooth between them, but it truly seemed like he loved her, despite their different political views.

A soft knock sounded at the door. I peeked through the peephole and saw Mandy's shock of red hair. She had an armful of cardboard takeout boxes. The two bodyguards stood sentinel at each side of the door.

I let her in and we dug into the food. They didn't have a steak salad, so Mandy chose a traditional Brazilian entrée for me—*feijoada*. To say it was delicious would be an understatement. I couldn't concentrate on anything except stuffing it in my face. Once I'd swallowed the last bite and licked the last of it off my spoon, I leaned back with a contented sigh.

We all looked up what we could about the Blondes on our smartphones as we ate, sharing the facts we discovered. We found a lot of articles in the local papers, and the story had even hit NPR.

The Blondes had been operating for two years and the local authorities were beyond frustrated. They had no leads. They didn't even know how many gang members there were. Up until now, they were more of an annoyance than anything else, taking well-off tourists for a few hours, spending their credit cards, and then letting them go. But things were changing.

Eddie looked up at me with pleading eyes. "They're doing this three to five times a week, according to the papers. If they start killing each target, that's a lot of dead bodies."

My stomach twisted at the thought of more women found in Dumpsters. We had diddly-squat to go on, and it didn't sound like the police had any more than we did. I had to find something, some clue, some person to lead me to them before they killed again.

# CHAPTER 13

IT WAS 4:30 A.M. by the time we made it back to our own hotel. Mandy crashed in her bed and was asleep in a matter of minutes. I couldn't sleep, even though I was exhausted. My brain would not shut off.

Taking the elevator to the fifth floor, I used my keycard to get into the hotel gym. It was larger then I thought it would be, and even had a punching bag in the corner. It wasn't a real one, just the kind on a plastic stand filled with sand or water, but it would do.

After stretching, I ran on the treadmill for ten minutes to warm up and then pushed the punching bag to the middle of the room. I was glad no one else was there. I had some pent-up energy to release, so this bag was in for a beating.

I started with a simple jab, jab, hook—then added an uppercut. After three minutes, I was sweating.

With each punch, I made sure to stay on the balls of my feet, knees bent, shifting from one foot to the other.

Strike, punch past the bag, pull hands back to chin, duck, come up with the uppercut.

I imagined the bag was a thug, an attacker. Hank Williams or one of his henchmen. Even though he was dead and buried, I felt my anger boil at the thought of his smug face.

Night and solitude did this to me—I gave my dark side free rein.

I was angry. Angry about a lot of things. Angry at men like Williams, angry that I had to deal with Dan and his advances, angry about my mom's phone call, angry that Tanya Lofton had died, and angry that Solomon was ignoring my texts.

What ever happened to a normal life? I lived in little Boise, Idaho. Nothing was supposed to happen in Boise. There was little to no crime and it was one of the top ten places to raise a family in the U.S. So why did all kinds of trouble follow me?

And the worst thought of all—why did I like it?

Sweat drenched my body. I left wet marks on the bag with each punch. Adding in some kicks, I poured all my power into my hips and relaxed my foot, giving each kick a whip-like action. Each kick tipped the bag on end, sloshing water in the bottom. Anger churned within me, but like running in the dark when I was scared, punishing this bag made the anger grow.

"Argh."

That's when I realized that it wasn't them: Hank, Dan, Solomon, or even Mom. I was mad at myself. It was this thing inside, a cloud that overshadowed everything. The dark side of myself. Something had broken loose. When I first felt it, I hated it. But with each passing day and each new criminal I met, I found myself getting used to it, even liking the way it made me feel safe.

It had kept me safe from Hank and Glen Williams. It had saved Angela. It couldn't be all bad, could it?

But the part that scared me was that I was hungry for more. I kept imagining ways to stop those that got away. Permanently.

Silent tears streamed down my cheeks and I fell to the floor. What was wrong with me? Why was I like this? I didn't hate people—I loved people, wanted to protect them. And yet I couldn't deny that something in me was different.

No, this wasn't me, not who I was. I wouldn't be that weak little girl ever again.

Getting to my feet, I wiped at my eyes and hit the bag. Jab, jab, hook. I was spent, exhausted and tired, but felt good.

I had no answers about how to deal with the dark side of myself, this primal urge to kill. But sometimes, even answers didn't fix things. Punching a bag in the early morning light was the closest to peace I'd get.

# CHAPTER 14

SOAKED IN SWEAT, I walked into my room to find Mandy sitting up in bed groggy-eyed. She looked at me and waved a hand toward the bathroom. "Solomon's in there. He wanted a shower."

I snorted. "Nice try. I'm covered in sweat and didn't sleep last night, so I get first dibs. You'll just have to wait, missy. You don't want me on the furniture until I've hosed off."

I pushed open the door, and steam billowed out of it. In the shower was a tall figure. A broad-shouldered, hairy-chested, completely naked man. I yelped and closed my eyes. "Ohmigod—"

Solomon turned and wiped the fogged-up shower door, grinning at me. "A little privacy, eh?"

"I, uh … what—?" I backed out and shut the door. Turning, I slid down the wall and covered my face.

"Told ya." Mandy giggled and threw a pillow at me. "You see anything?"

"No. I mean, yes. But the glass … foggy."

"Bummer. You should really check out the assets before you make your relationship official."

My face burned. I couldn't remember the last time I'd been this embarrassed. Here I was, sweaty, in my ratty gym clothes, and *that's* when Solomon decides to show up? Why not last night, when I looked cute? I glared at Mandy. A good wing woman never would have let him through the door. "How did he get here?"

"Well, Sarah Renee Steele …" I knew she was trying to be a pain by the way she said my full name. "I'm sure he took a plane. It would be quite a hike otherwise."

"Mandy!"

"Okay, okay. He said the FBI got called in on some case and he can't check into his room until one or something. And he *had* to see you."

I was a little lost. "FBI?"

He spoke from behind the bathroom door, making me jump. "Oh, I meant to tell you. I work for the FBI."

My head swam at that, and not just because I was still hot from my workout. The realization that I was so close to someone in law enforcement floored me. I searched my memory for every time we had been together, trying to figure out if I had slipped at all. I didn't think I had. We hadn't spoken about a lot of personal things, so I hadn't dropped any clues about my past. Grabbing the pillow, I put my face in it and swore at the top of my lungs. I'd been reckless. I never should have gotten close to a man who was such a mystery.

But still, it wasn't all my fault. He'd lied to me.

I knocked my elbow against the wall in disgust. "Guess they don't teach you tact at the FBI."

"Guess they don't teach you how to knock at law school," he retorted.

I crossed my arms and glared at Mandy. "Guess I need a new friend who won't let lying men into the room without my permission."

"I never lied," he said through the door.

"You said you were a consultant."

"I am. I never said I wasn't FBI."

Liar. It was what he *didn't* say that worried me. What else wasn't he telling me?

Mandy flopped her head on her pillow. "Don't blame me. I was asleep, he knocked and woke me, and blah blah blah, told me his story. He wanted to get a shower because he was stuck on a plane all night. You should be happy to see him, but you're acting crazy. I knew you liked him, but dang, girl." I set my jaw at that. She sleepily mumbled, "Now get out of those butt-ugly workout clothes and into some jeans. How long have you owned those? Since freshman year?"

I looked down at my clothes. She was right. I'd had them since college. Looking under my arms, I noticed sweat stains and a not-so-pleasant aroma. Yeesh. "I think I need to go shopping." I scrambled for my suitcase, hurrying before Solomon came out.

"And you need to donate those clothes to the CDC. I'm sure they could discover some new bacterial life forms on them."

I peeled off my shirt and threw it at her. She ducked under the covers.

I rummaged through my suitcase, pulled off my workout pants, and yanked on jeans. I was in the middle of putting on my shirt, with my arms up and over my head when I heard the bathroom door open. *You've got to be kidding me.*

I twisted around and awkwardly pulled the shirt down. I tried to play it cool. "Care to explain yourself, Special Agent Solomon?"

But he didn't let me get away with it. "You walk in on me, I walk in on you. Hey, Mandy, maybe you should pull off that blanket just so we're all even."

"Ha. Nice try, FBI." She pulled the blanket up to her chest. "You'd be so lucky."

I hugged myself, feeling very silly and a little flushed. I glanced up at Solomon to find him shirtless, with a white towel around his waist.

He looked good—more than good. I mean, wow.

"I need my bag." Solomon maneuvered past me with a coy smile on his face. "I'll just get this and change in the bathroom. Give me five minutes."

It was still hard to believe he was here. But when he came close, I could smell his unmistakable man-scent and see the way his skin glistened with water… all I wanted to do was jump him. Speaking through gritted teeth, I said, "You should leave until I cool down."

"Do I make you that hot?"

Was I that see-through? "No! I'm pissed. Get out of here before I punch you in the face."

Solomon nodded and grabbed his bag. "Got it. I'll explain everything once we're all dressed and have had some breakfast." He looked at Mandy. "Is she always this crabby in the morning?"

Mandy nodded.

I narrowed my eyes at him. "Breakfast? Not on your life. I'm giving you ten minutes—that's all."

"Fair enough. Just see what I can do with ten minutes." He shut the bathroom door, and I turned to Mandy and groaned.

"Nice, Sarah. Attack him first thing."

"He can't just barge into our space, our time, announce that he's FBI—"

"That's what really gets you, right? His secrets."

I stood still and silent, thinking. "No, it's not the secrets. I'll always keep secrets and I expect others to."

"Then what is it?"

I pulled my ring on and off my finger, fidgeting. I opened my mouth to respond when I realized he could hear everything we said. Snapping my mouth closed, I motioned with my eyes toward the door and Mandy understood.

"Will you listen to him?" Her voice was soft, compassionate.

I nodded.

But that didn't mean I'd let him stay. I made it a personal policy never to be a bed partner with law enforcement. At the memory of what I had seen in the shower, I almost made an exception. But no, I had to stick to my principles. No matter what his abs looked like.

# CHAPTER 15

AFTER SOLOMON GOT OUT of the bathroom, I went in and locked the door. I took an extra-long shower. I watched the water flow down the drain and let my trouble go. I relaxed my muscles, massaged my neck, and tried to regain perspective.

Using extra lather, I rubbed the foamy washcloth extra hard over my skin. By the time I stepped, dripping, onto the towel, I smelled like a garden. But I put on some fresh-scented lotion for good measure.

Wiping the mirror, I noticed that my hair was even more blonde than normal. The sun was bleaching it.

"Hurry up in there," Mandy bellowed from the bedroom. "I'm hungry."

"Hold your horses." So she decided to skip the shower and do breakfast first. That meant they were waiting on me. Let them wait.

It would be hot out, so I opted for a loose skirt, light blue T-shirt, and sandals. After my killer makeup skills, aka putting on clear lip gloss, I opened the bathroom door. "Everyone decent?"

Solomon stood and looked me up and down. If any other man did that to me I would be miffed, but when he did it, I liked how it felt. I stiffened against the feelings. Why'd he have to surprise me like this?

When he reached to hug me, I shouldered past him. He gently grabbed my forearm.

I gritted my teeth.

"I've never seen you mad before."

"It's usually the last thing a person sees," I said with a wry smile.

"Oh, yeah?"

"Yeah."

"So, where are we going to eat?" Mandy cut in.

I sighed. "I don't care—just get me food."

Solomon picked up a hotel pamphlet. "Why not the lobby? I thought I saw a cafè."

Nodding, I said, "Sounds good."

They surged to the door. I squared my shoulders and leveled my gaze, ready to break up with Solomon.

# CHAPTER 16

THE POOR EGGS HAD no chance under the mighty power of Mandy and her deathly fork. I would have been embarrassed by how she was attacking her breakfast, but it was Mandy.

She finished her omelet before I even received my French toast. She stood, scraping her chair back. "I'm off. I'll let you two stew whatever recipe you have going here."

I turned in surprise. "Mandy."

But she'd already turned away. "I'll be checking to see if we can afford parasailing," she said as she walked off.

The waiter brought my steaming French toast with a pool of butter in the middle. I didn't cut into it, which should have given Solomon an idea of how serious I was. Solomon had ordered oatmeal with a side of bacon. Who orders oatmeal in Rio? It convinced me even more that our relationship would not work out, no matter how much I was attracted to him.

"Okay. Spill it, bud."

Solomon grinned. When he did, the corners of his eyes crinkled. It was cute. *Focus, Sarah. Keep on point.*

He took a bite out of a thick slice of bacon, chewed, and

swallowed. "I'm FBI. Can't tell you much more than that."

"Well then, I'm not going to play around with you. It's been fun, but it's over."

He took a sip of water and looked at me out of the corner of his eye. "You want your man to tell you everything?"

I winced. "You're not my man. And I'm a big fan of keeping secrets. I just don't want to be with someone whose sole job is to find them out. Can't tell you much more than that." I repeated his words back to him.

"That sounds suspicious." He squared his shoulders. I wasn't sure if he was joking or not. "What secrets do you need kept from the law?"

A good lie is one you never have to tell. Many people in trouble lie to save themselves, but every now and again, the real con artist will tell you the flat-out truth and bank that you won't believe them. It works especially well when paired with humor.

"I'm a killer. I shot a man in Reno just to watch him die."

He looked at me soberly. "No wonder I'm so drawn to you. You're a Johnny Cash fan."

I crossed my arms.

"I like you," he said, digging into his oatmeal.

I almost left at that. Breaking ties with him was turning out to be harder than I'd expected. Instead, I poured syrup over my French toast—so much that the bread was almost floating on my plate. My workout had famished me.

Just as I lifted the first bite to my lips, Solomon said, "Do you mean you're a killer because you shot Hank Williams and his muscleman, or …" he lowered his voice, "the fact that your mother claims you murdered your own father?"

I had gotten so good at masking my emotions that I didn't even blink at the words. Those hurts had been buried deep, but to hear Solomon say it made my heart beat so much faster. I chewed slowly.

I didn't even taste it. I squeezed the arm of my chair so tight, my knuckles turned white.

We ate in silence. I don't know if he'd said that to get a rise out of me or if he expected me to pour my heart out to him. But I gave him nothing.

I had already mapped my exit and was ready to bolt. However, since I had the FBI sitting beside me, I might as well take advantage of it and ask about the Blondes. It was the only good thing I could draw from this encounter. I wanted to give Eddie some answers. Then I'd walk out of Solomon's life forever.

As opposed to last time, I shot straight.

"Have any leads in the Tanya Lofton case?"

He didn't miss a beat. "The authorities think it's the Blondes, but they have no evidence besides Eddie's word that two blonde girls were the ones who kidnapped her."

"The Blondes … you mean that group you warned me about?"

"Yes. And don't play dumb. We heard you helped Mr. Lofton and already know half as much about the gang as I do."

"Oh, really?" I fidgeted with my napkin, twisting it around my finger. "Don't be modest. I probably only know one-third of the things you do." Then I cut down to what I wanted from him. "Why'd they change their M.O.?"

"Gangs like these evolve. There's the law of diminishing returns. Stealing isn't getting them as high as it used to."

"You think it's all psychological, not at all financial?"

He took another bite of his oatmeal. It looked so dry next to my French toast. The poor guy obviously made bad choices.

He shrugged. He didn't want to tell me any more. "Mr. Lofton will be escorted back to the States. It seems that the local authorities aren't going to break the case, so we're unofficially stepping in."

"Unofficially? What does that mean?" I leaned toward him.

He lowered his voice. "It means, not confirmed officially."

"Don't be a brat."

Giving a wry grin, he said, "The FBI wasn't asked to help out, so we are here under the embassy's authority, as consultants. We can do almost everything we need to, but when it comes down to it, the local police will have to make arrests."

"How's Eddie doing?"

"He's resting, supposed to be flying out later this afternoon. I do need to take your official statement, but for now you can just tell me what happened."

"Sure."

Solomon frowned. "Now, Sarah, I really need you to leave this alone. The FBI is taking this seriously and I don't want you involved. You are here on vacation. I can't do my job if I'm worried about your safety."

I didn't know what to say, or what I really thought. Up until now, Mandy and Joshua had been the only ones who looked out for me. For a second I enjoyed the feeling of being protected by a big, tall, strong agent. And then reality hit and burst my bubble. He probably had an angle.

So I lied. "I'll stay out of it. I trust you and your FBI'ing abilities."

"Good. That's a load off my mind." He searched my face and shook his head as if he knew I was lying. I pertly patted my lips with my napkin. He didn't have any say in my life. If Eddie wanted my help, I would give it.

He leaned forward so his hair fell on his forehead. He brushed it back, and a waft of his shampoo came my way. God, he smelled good. "Now, what happened?"

# CHAPTER 17

SOLOMON TOOK NOTES AS I recounted my interaction with Eddie in the parking lot and his hotel room, leaving out anything that implied I wanted to get involved. He ordered us two lattes, and we sipped them as I talked.

Right as I finished, Mandy walked up. "I booked our surfboard and parasailing adventures."

"Have you found your homeless child to adopt yet?"

Mandy snorted. "Not yet."

Solomon looked up from his cup. "What?"

"Nothing," I said. "What time's our first challenge?"

"Four. I bought an underwater camera too. So we can chronicle our trip."

We talked as if Solomon wasn't there. It brought me some amused satisfaction.

I stood and Mandy linked her arm through mine. "Let's go shopping before then."

"Okay. But before we hit all that, this girl needs some sleep."

Mandy yawned as if on cue. "Yeah, I got, like, two hours and could use a few more. How about we head back to the room and get going around noon?"

Closing his notebook, Solomon nodded. "Great. I love being invisible. Just what an agent should be. I'll text you when I'm free, if you guys want to grab dinner later."

He was incorrigible. "No, thanks." I kissed Solomon on the forehead as if he were a little kid. "Just stay away."

He bowed his head. "I'm nothing if not obedient to a beautiful girl's wishes. Goodbye. Be good." His words put me on edge—why was he so accepting of my rejection? He didn't seem like the kind of guy who would squall about it, but still, he didn't even mention it.

I let him have the last word. With a little smile, I turned and walked away. No doubt we'd run into him again, but if I was lucky, I wouldn't have to speak to him.

And then I marveled at my ability of self-deception.

# CHAPTER 18

I DIDN'T REALIZE HOW exhausted I was until I lay down. The long night, my intense workout, my mind battering me, and seeing Solomon all amounted to one tired girl.

I woke up still on top of the covers with one shoe barely on and the other missing. Bending down, I found it under the bed and then noticed the time—after one in the afternoon. So much for starting our day at noon.

Mandy was snoring and had one hand draped over her face. I decided to let her sleep and go hit the gym. I could feel the stir of whatever slept inside. It needed out, and one of the best ways was a good hard workout. Not that I needed another one today, but I had to do something. I ended up just doing some push-ups and sit-ups, but it felt good to move some energy.

Twenty minutes later, I was spent, but felt better. Mandy was still out like a hibernating bear. I wanted to freshen up, so I stepped into the bathroom.

Turned out my hair had made it through my mini workout. I brushed my teeth, changed into shorts and an athletic tank, and braided my hair.

After I considered splashing water on Mandy's face and then rejected the idea because I valued our friendship, I decided on a much nicer way to wake her.

Taking out one of my pens, I started drawing a rose tattoo on her forearm. She stirred. "Rise and shine, sleepyhead." Her arm twitched, and just as I finished the last leaf, she bolted up. She yanked her arm away and gasped.

"You ruined me."

"Ha. It'd take a lot more ink than that."

She scrubbed at her arm and then gave me a glare that had a smile simmering behind it. I pushed her legs off the bed. "You said noon, not one. Noon, Mandy. You still have so much to cross off your list."

She groaned and rolled over, pulling her legs up under her. "Go away, demon spawn. I take back what I said. Lists are terrible ideas on vacation."

I shoved her off the bed and laughed when she cursed.

"Come on, I'm all dressed." Mandy didn't move. "I look hot," I teased.

"You always look hot. Now go away."

"Fine. I'm going down to get a coffee—text me when you're coming. And don't go back to sleep or we can't shop. You know how badly I need new clothes."

Taking a room key card, I put it in my purse and walked to the elevator. I had at least an hour to kill, as Mandy was not the fastest riser.

This day was going nowhere fast, but that was fine with me. Walking the four-hundred yards to the beach, I took off my shoes and casually strolled in the sand. I couldn't get enough of the ocean air, the sand between my toes, and the sight of the greenest mountains I'd ever seen. Palm trees lined the beach, and their leaves rustled in the salty breeze. The sun warmed my skin and I couldn't help the smile tugging my lips. Being outside was good for the soul.

A little tiki hut stood to my left and I smelled something delicious. My mouth started watering when I saw what the man was serving.

"Three shots of espresso, a little cream, and a shot of coconut," I ordered. Most of the people here spoke English. It made sense—this was a tourist trap built just for us.

Marco, our valet driver from the hotel, waved at me from across the street and I took my coffee to go.

"Hey, Marco. You working all day today?"

"Yes, Miss Steele, all day. You going out, see the sites?"

"Maybe. Mandy's taking her time so I'm down here again, waiting like a dutiful wife."

"Miss Steele, you a dutiful wife? Hm. I no judge." Marco shook his head and I laughed, letting him know it was just an English expression.

Marco took my hand and held it out to inspect me. "You a sweet lady. You remind me of my daughter. She your age."

"Well, thank you, Marco."

"Very good, Miss Steele. I tell your friend where to find you when she comes down?"

"No, thanks. She'll text when she's on her way. Have a good one."

"Good, good. You need anything, or you want someone to take you to see the real Rio, you give me a call?"

I winked at him and walked on.

The espresso was good, but as soon as I drank it, I remembered the time. To my body it was morning, but outside it was the middle of the day, and hot. I started to sweat, and looking out at the ocean made me want to go for a swim.

Tossing the empty coffee cup in a trash bin, I turned to find myself standing in front of Eddie Lofton's hotel. Checking the time on my cell and not seeing a text from Mandy, I decided to go see how Eddie was doing. Maybe the FBI had discovered some new information on the case.

# CHAPTER 19

AS I CROSSED THE lobby, I noticed two men reading newspapers in the plush chairs. My eyes roved past and then went back to them. One had a slight bulge just under his shoulder, and the other had a cane beside him. That, paired with the way they watched the door and their lack of attention to their papers, convinced me they were feds. I wondered if Solomon was watching me now. As I waited for the elevator, I looked at my phone again and sighed. Dang that girl—she must have fallen asleep again.

The elevator doors opened. I stepped inside and hit the correct button. A man in bike shorts punched in a higher floor. As it's impossible not to look when someone's wearing bike shorts, I checked him out. His build was muscular and athletic, except for his chubby baby cheeks. He seemed like the kind of guy who only wore organic clothing and ate seeds and berries. I was about to make small talk when he ripped one. Just like that. I scrunched my nose and tried not to breathe. The smell saturated the air, and I gagged. The elevator seemed smaller and slower than any elevator I'd ever been in. By the time we reached the fourth floor, I was praying. *God, if I get out of this alive, I swear I'll start volunteering at a soup kitchen.* I watched the floor numbers tick by.

The doors finally opened and I fell out, sucking air. No way was I ever getting on an elevator again with a protein-munching guy in bike shorts. Too risky.

Regaining my composure, I walked toward Eddie's room. A pretty blonde girl with jet-black eyes was coming down the hall and for a second I imagined her to be one of the gang. That was a weird thought. Perhaps it was because her dress and boots were a designer label and looked right off the shelf. Or maybe I just had an overactive imagination.

She avoided eye contact as we passed. I turned left down a short hall and knocked on Eddie's door. A minute later, the door opened. Eddie Lofton greeted me and smiled, even though his eyes were groggy and he looked like he was still in the clothes we left him in last night.

"Sarah."

"Can I come in?"

He nodded and I stepped forward, wishing I could make this all go away and that Mr. and Mrs. Lofton could go on to fix their marriage and live their lives together.

Something ground under my heel and I looked down. A gold chain glinted in the carpet. I picked up the necklace and examined it.

Eddie snatched it from my hands. "This is hers … this is Tanya's necklace. She was wearing it when she was taken." He looked at me and blinked as if trying to figure out how it came to be in my hand. He had an unmistakable air of distrust about him. "Where did you get it?"

"I stepped on it. It was on the floor—"

It must have been the girl I passed in the hallway. She left it!

I turned and ran down the short hall and toward the elevators. The doors were just closing and I glimpsed the blonde girl standing inside. Reeling to a halt, I punched the down button, but I knew I was too late. And by the time another elevator came, she would be long gone.

I took the stairs two at a time and crashed through the first-floor door. I knew it was her—my gut told me. She'd come to give it back, but why?

The lobby was filled with people—new people checking in and guests checking out. The agents were still in the chairs. They'd let her pass right by. That was okay—I wanted to handle it myself.

I scanned the crowd as I ran, but didn't see her. I headed straight for the front door.

Pushing past a bellhop, who yelled after me—sweet words, I'm sure—I stopped and turned, looking for the small girl in the crowd. Heat slammed into me and my lungs burned.

There, past the palm tree. I saw her shiny hair glint in the sun. I ran toward her and she looked over her shoulder. This time she made eye contact—and then she ran.

# CHAPTER 20

THE GIRL TURNED DOWN an alley, and I started to panic. I would lose her—the only lead, one of the actual gang members—because she was faster than me. It was the stairs. They'd done me in. I promised myself I'd start working on the StairMaster when I got back home.

Gasping for air, I pushed down the pain forming in my left lung. Giving up was not in me, at least not yet. I'd track her urban-style if I had to. I was on the hunt now. I rounded the corner and saw that it was a dead-end alley. My hopes soared.

The blonde girl had a lock-pick set out. She was trying to pick a locked metal door. When she saw me, she dropped the tools and put her fists up. She backed up to a brick wall.

"Hey, just calm down. I want to talk—I won't hurt you." My breath came in gasps, which I tried to hide by evening out my breathing. I positioned myself between the wall and a large Dumpster. In order to get past me, she would have to squeeze by me. I could grab her if I needed to.

The girl was sweating, and she shifted from foot to foot. She ran her hands through her damp hair and we stared at each other like two cats trying to size the other up.

"Look, I just need to know why you brought the necklace back. I'm his friend and I need some answers."

She shook her head. Her fists were still in position, and I noticed she had good form. I expected her to attack me, maybe lash out or pull a knife. My hand went into my purse and my fingers wrapped around a keychain can of mace spray. But she didn't move. Instead, she bit her lower lip.

I relaxed my stance and softened my eyes. "Do you speak English?"

"Yes."

"Did you bring the necklace back?"

She nodded.

"Why?"

She paused, and that's when I saw her regret behind the mask she wore. "She deserved better. Never should've got shot."

"Who shot her?"

"Not me—I just snag and grab. Thought it would always be that way. Things are changing. I just wanted him to have it back … Tell him I'm sorry."

"I can help get you out." I took a step forward, and she launched to one side and bolted past me. I grabbed for her shoulder and got her purse strap. In a split second, I made a decision. It'd be easier to secure a bag than a human, so I decided to keep holding the purse at the risk of losing her. She punched at my stomach, but I easily dodged and tightened my hold on her purse. Twisting free of it, she ran down the alley.

She rounded the corner. I stood holding her small handbag, wondering if I should chase after her.

I didn't think she would tell me any more, but it would have been good to bring her in and let Solomon question her. By that time I decided it was too late. And I was tired.

The high sun made heat waves on the concrete. I looked after her. What had she gotten herself into?

# CHAPTER 21

EDDIE LOFTON SAT ON the edge of his bed and stared at his hands. The golden pendant dangled from his fingers.

Mandy was on her way up. I told her I'd fill her in once she got here. I dialed Solomon and he picked up after the first ring.

"Hey, what's up?"

"You should come to Mr. Lofton's hotel right away."

Solomon sighed. "Sarah, I told you to let me handle this. What did you do?"

"It's not my fault. Right place, right time. Besides, this is a lead, and you need all the leads you can get."

"You are a magnet for problems, aren't you?" I picked up a hint of teasing in his voice.

"Just get over here."

"Okay. Try to stay out of trouble till I get there."

"No promises." I hung up and there was a knock at the door. I let Mandy in, and she looked me up and down and snorted.

"Wow, what did you do to yourself?"

Looking in the mirror, I saw that my hair was a frizz fest, and it was clear that I had been sweating up a storm. "Went for a run. I have something to show you."

She peered into the bedroom. "How's he doing?"

"I think he's in shock. He should get home to America as soon as he can."

Mandy plopped down on the sofa. She looked and sounded nonchalant, but I could tell this meant something to her by the way she cased the joint when she walked in.

I filled her in. "I was going for a walk, sipping my espresso, waiting for this annoying so-called best friend, when I decided to stop in and see how Eddie was doing."

"Annoying *and* smokin'-hot best friend."

"Sure, whatever. On the way up, I passed this blonde girl in the hall."

"Uh-oh, I see where this is going." Mandy's eyes went sharp as she thought. "Why would one of them return?"

"An attack of conscience." When I said it, it brought me some hope. If one of them had the fear of God eating away at them, the chances of finding them were much greater than if they'd all been going in the same direction.

"So she ran, I chased, and got this." I held up the purse.

"Hers?" Mandy said.

"No, I snatched it from some stranger," I scoffed. "Of course it's hers. Here, wear these." I handed her some latex gloves. I put mine on and laughed at the moronic look she was giving me. "What? I borrowed them from the house-cleaning cart."

Once we had our gloves on, I dumped the contents of the purse on the small desk. The purse was a small cream deal with a flower on one side. It looked like Coach and Mandy confirmed it by whistling.

"Dang, this is a spendy bag. It could be a knockoff, but I doubt it. Was she dressed in designer clothing?"

"Yes. She looked like any other tourist. Not overdone. She blended in."

"Guess she would if she was smart. So, what do we have here? Makeup, high end. Little mirror. Travel Kleenexes. Two tampons. The usual girl stuff."

I flipped open a wallet and found a pre-paid Visa card, but no ID. "She sure is careful. Cell phone is prepaid, and so is the debit card. Guess we could find out who they're registered to. No ID, nothing to lead back to her."

Mandy dug through a small notebook and a receipt fell out. I picked it up and looked at the address, and then I pulled out my cell and took a picture of the receipt and the contents of the purse.

"So does this mean we can go shopping now?" Mandy waved the card in the air. "It seems I suddenly came into some money."

"It'd serve them right, but no. This has to go to Solomon."

"Wow, you're no fun at all."

# CHAPTER 22

VITORIA KNEW THE MURDER had rattled the girls. They'd had no idea it was coming and it would take some work to get them to see her side. But she lived by the adage, "It's easier to apologize than ask for permission."

They ate the takeout Emilia had picked up. Everyone ate silently, giving Vitoria furtive glances.

In the gentlest voice she had, Vitoria began. "I started this so we could have a future, not live in the muck of the slums like a bunch of second-rate degenerates. I dragged you out of the trash and now look at you—wearing Prada and sipping drinks more expensive than your *papai's* weekly salary." She needed to appeal to their past. "Mia—you'd never have left your pimp if not for me. Lili—you were bored out of your mind at that girls school. And Emilia—" Her voice lowered. "Your boyfriend would still be using you as a punching bag every night if you hadn't escaped. We have a good thing here … a good family. Don't let it go."

Their eyes had softened at her words, at the memories she'd invoked.

Mia, her right-hand girl, spoke up first. One word. "Why?"

Vitoria spoke quickly. "Money. Why else? That's why I've been taking trips to America. By doing this one simple job today, we made twice as much money as we have the whole time we've been working. Take a few of these jobs and we can get out of here. Live the high life in New York or New Orleans—"

"Or Las Vegas, baby," Lili interrupted. She really had no clue what was going on.

"But this is on you. I need you all behind me. I'm not messing around anymore. You have to start taking this seriously."

"We do, Vit, but I never wanted this," Emilia said. Out of them all, Vitoria expected the most trouble from goody-two-shoes Emilia. She was a softie.

"Things are different now." How was Vitoria supposed to tell them this little operation was not what they thought it was, that she only gave them one-fifth of all the money she made, and she was working for some very powerful people? There was some hardcore pressure involved. If they didn't keep their word, they'd have more than cops after their tail.

She softened her tone. "We were kids when we started. We aren't kids anymore—time we acted like it."

Mia stood up and stretched. "As long as you keep splitting it up even, I'll always have your back." She walked over and gripped Vitoria by the shoulder. Everyone tensed. "But if you *ever* pull one on us like this again, I'm out."

Vitoria nodded, staring her down until she let go.

Emilia crossed her arms over her chest and glared at Vitoria.

"Got something to say?" Vitoria asked.

"Yeah. This started as a team—all of us in as equals, and we were supposed to talk about everything. Who made you the leader?"

Vitoria managed to keep her cool, even though this little brat had no idea how much went into making things work. "You think you can do better? Fine, you pick the marks. You work out a price with the buyers and make sure we don't get ripped off. Be my guest."

Emilia looked up at Mia and then back to Vitoria. "I wasn't saying that—just that we should all be in the loop."

"No, you *were* saying that. If you don't trust me, then go. No one will stop you. But if you want to step up, I suggest you keep your trap shut."

Vitoria turned and walked out the back door and into the night. Her face felt hot, and her hands were shaking. Who did Emilia think she was to challenge her like that? If anyone was the weakest team member, it was Emilia. She didn't know half of it, and Vitoria would keep it that way. As *Avó* told her, "Never tell all or you'll be stuck with nothing."

Closing her eyes, she let a deep breath fill her lungs, then let it out on a ten count. The back of the warehouse was overgrown with weeds and vines. A few yards past a rusted-out VW bus was a small outhouse, or what used to be one.

Vitoria pulled her new Glock .45 from her shoulder holster and checked the chamber. After taking the lock off the van door, she opened it. The hinges screamed in protest.

It was dark, but the moon was full so she could clearly see the two women inside. They were tied and gagged, a mother-daughter duo. The two wriggled and moaned when they saw the door open, but it wouldn't do them any good. They were dead already—they just didn't know it.

# CHAPTER 23

WE WERE ON OUR way to go surfing. I pulled a knit dress up over my hips and used it to cover my bikini. Stepping into sandals, I was once again waiting on Mandy.

"Are you taking another hour to get ready just to end up wet and salty?"

"Now that sounds like a good time. But no, I'm just about done."

Clicking on the TV, I found a local station and read the subtitles. A storm was coming the day after tomorrow, but today would have perfect weather.

"Have any news on my dragon bracelet?"

"I swept the room again, but didn't find it. The next thing to do is search the bellhop's locker. Although she probably wouldn't be stupid enough to keep it there—who knows." I was teasing Mandy, but she thought I was serious. I wouldn't search some poor maid's locker because my best friend lost her bracelet.

"You should do that now."

"I should do that after we surf. Come on. We'll be late."

Mandy shut off the bathroom light and stood in all her bikini-clad glory. She never bothered with swimsuit cover-ups. She said that if people saw it on the beach, they could see it on the way *to* the beach.

I said something that had been bothering me since the talk with Solomon. "Do you think he just didn't tell me to keep me safe?"

Mandy knew exactly which *he* I was referring to. "Of course. Solomon's with the FBI, for goodness' sake. So I'm sure he wants you out of harm's way."

"I'm not a damsel in distress."

"I know. But take it as a compliment. Relationships are really hard for agents. Haven't you seen James Bond? Even *starting* a relationship means he really likes you."

I crinkled my nose. "Well, this is much deeper now. This isn't about me or him—it's about justice. The Blondes have murdered two people so far, and who knows how many more will die if someone doesn't stop them."

"I know, Sarah, but this isn't your job. You're not a detective or a cop."

I just wanted to know why they started killing their victims. Was someone forcing these women to kill?

My train of thought broke when Mandy motioned toward the TV. A reporter stood in front of a small rundown house. In the background, police and emergency workers milled about.

Mandy sat heavily on the bed and turned up the volume. Even though we couldn't understand the language, we read the subtitles. "They found two more bodies. A mother and daughter…"

I looked at Mandy and my skin tingled. "They were found in the same area of the slums where Mrs. Lofton was discovered. That could be their home base."

"Looks that way. That's four deaths. So now what?"

"We go surfing and then we follow up with the receipt I got from the girl's purse. Oh, and we try not to get kidnapped by the Blondes."

# CHAPTER 24

"HERE IT COMES—THIS TIME I'm staying up." Mandy was next to me on a hot-pink surfboard. We took the hour lesson and then decided to go at it alone; the young instructor seemed to know less than we did about surfing. The next wave was huge, so I readied the underwater camera Mandy had bought and clicked a picture just as she stood on the board. A second later, her foot slipped and she went face-first into the wave. Gasping for air, she scrambled back on her board and asked me eagerly, "Did you get it?"

"You mean, did I get you standing on the board for that split second?"

"Yes."

I chuckled. "Yes, I got it. Rick will be so impressed."

Another wave was coming. I tied the camera to my wrist and readied myself for the hit.

Mandy called to me over the sound of the surf. "I'm gonna beat you this time."

"Sure, when manta rays fly. I'll try not to show you up too bad." I hadn't known what to expect when we first started, but I was blown away by how much I liked surfing.

"I can't help it if I'm better suited for a Harley than standing on a stupid board," she said.

The weather report showed that the big storm would hit late tomorrow morning, which meant the waves all day today and early tomorrow would be killer. The water was peppered with surfers, but I felt like we were the only tourists. After the news hit about the murders, there was a rush at the airports. Basically, all the rich foreigners were leaving. The resort and the entire coastline looked like it was in the middle of winter instead of the height of tourist season. This would hurt the whole town.

"Here it comes." I started paddling toward the shore. As the water rose, I got to my knees, stood, and caught the front side. Picking up speed, I kept my knees bent to adjust. I turned to match the angle of the curve and saw Mandy stand, then slip and fall. I choked on a laugh.

Shifting my weight, I leaned to the inside and wind blew my hair behind me. It was crazy fun. For a moment I forgot all about Solomon and the Blondes. The top of the wave broke around me and I kept my edge. The wave flattened out and I went to my knees, then turned to find Mandy. She tried to paddle to shore, but she kept getting swept away from land. I should have put her on a leash.

I headed toward the beach, reached it, and stuck my board in the sand as if I was conquering the land.

It was beautiful out and I was hungry. Mandy wanted to go for a hike up to the famous statue Cristo Redentor later, and I needed some calories. Digging through my beach bag, all I found was a hard candy. It would have to do.

Mandy was still pretty far from shore, so I flopped onto my huge, cushiony beach towel and the sand molded underneath me like a bed. Starting at my shoulders, I consciously relaxed all my muscles, melting into the fabric. The sun kissed my cheeks, warming them. I vaguely heard the sound of seagulls and children's play, but it didn't sink in. I concentrated on … nothing.

But then a thought blew in and splattered in my mind like unruly paint. It had been niggling in there since I'd heard what the Blondes did to Tanya, and now it saturated my peaceful rest. I tried to shut it down, tried to think back to nothing, but the thought was there and wouldn't leave.

The Blondes deserved justice.

And I should give it to them.

Unbidden plans of how I could track them down came to mind. Flashes of surprising them in their lair, disarming them, and then … I closed my eyes against the violence. That wasn't me. I had to put that side to rest.

But my peace had been shattered. I couldn't stay still any longer or the thoughts would return. I sat up, shading my eyes against the sun, and saw Mandy still paddling her way to the shore. Very awkwardly, I might add.

My phone beeped. Eager for the distraction, I picked it up, thinking it might be Eddie or Solomon. It was Joshua, my intern in Boise.

"Hello," I said brightly.

"Hi, Sarah," he said, and I could hear the smile behind his voice. Joshua was three hundred pounds of pure Samoan muscles. He could probably wrestle a great white shark and win. And he was one of the most trustworthy, dedicated people I'd ever worked with. He kept me focused on my tasks. It was good to have him in my corner.

"I found something for you," he said in his gentle voice.

"That's what I like to hear. Get results or you get the road," I said in a mock gruff voice.

"You couldn't find your car in the parking lot without me."

"Yeah, yeah—I want you, I need you, and all that jazz. What's the information?"

"Eddie Lofton. He won in a landslide against Rob Pearlman, who's run against him every election since then and really wants his seat back. But the people love Eddie, and it looks like he does right by them. He's never associated with any corporation, or even unions. He gives out his number on his website and takes calls from anyone. He listens to the voice of the people, and apparently acts on it."

"That's the fairy tale. What's the reality?"

Joshua paused. "At first I didn't find any big bad wolf, but after some stalwart digging into his past and a call or two to his office, I found that the next two bills he's pushing are regarding green energy. And they greatly favor a certain type of energy that only one company possesses."

"What company?"

"Williams, Inc."

My stomach dropped. Based in Boise, they were one of the most powerful energy companies in the country. I'd recently gotten really friendly with them when I was in charge of prosecuting their owner, Hank Williams, for kidnapping, rape, and murder. His daughter, Hannah Williams, now ran the company. And from the times we'd talked, I'd gotten the impression she was just as ruthless as Williams. In a less-bloody, more white-collar kind of way.

"Is Eddie golfing buddies with anyone at Williams?"

"Nope. If he has a connection with Williams, nobody's seen it. However..." his voice lit up, "his wife, may she rest in peace, was suing Williams Inc. for three different violations of health and environment code. She blogged about the unjust way they treat their employees, posted pictures of the harm they did to a camp in South America, and in an interview, she even said her life mission was to shut them down."

That was very interesting. Williams, Inc. had a lot to gain by Tanya's death. No one else in her small office would probably pick the case back up.

"That's good," I murmured. "Remind me to get you a raise."

"And dental?"

"Don't push it," I said.

"Hey, hurry home. I don't like being here in the office without you. I'm afraid of lawyers."

"Lawyers are jerks," I said. "Watch your back."

"You got it."

I hung up, thoughtful, sifting through the information Joshua had given me. Out of the corner of my eye, I saw Mandy approach.

"I hate you." Mandy dragged her board up, looking exhausted.

"I know. At least I got a picture of you upright. Don't worry—you can't be good at everything. I suck at computer-hacking stuff, and you're a wizard at it."

Mandy dropped down next to me and closed her eyes. We dozed off and on … or, more accurately, I *pretended* to doze off and on.

Then Mandy shocked me by saying, "Do you think they suffered?"

Sitting up, I turned to her. "Who?"

"The ladies they killed. I mean, the file said Mrs. Lofton had been assaulted."

"How did you know that?"

"I looked at the report."

"You hacked the FBI database?"

"No, stupid. I'm not a real magician, nor do I want to be a felon. I accidentally logged into Eddie's email, as he was connected to the hotel's Wi-Fi. Then I accidently saw a report the police had sent him to answer his questions. It said that Nancy had a burn mark on her arm and her face was battered. And it said Tanya had multiple contusions on her body and face, plus a fractured arm."

I imagined for a second what the victims went through, and was pulled away from reality. I didn't feel the sun on my back or the wind on my cheeks anymore. "Someone's behind all this. I wonder if the leader has been corrupted by an outsider." Then I told her what Joshua had discovered.

Mandy ran a hand through her hair. "I really wanted to just chill, be on vacation, but I can't get them out of my head. I close my eyes and see their bodies …"

That was normal. When I closed *my* eyes, I saw the Blondes' bodies. Which made me a psycho freak.

Mandy said seriously, "So, can we sneak out, lie to our parents, and get into trouble?"

"That about sums it up. And when you say 'parents,' I assume you're talking about Solomon."

"Okay, just let me tan for an hour first. I need to get a good one so when we go back home, I can make everyone jealous."

"You've got to sort out your priorities."

# CHAPTER 25

"HEY, MARCO." I WALKED up to him and held out a hundred-dollar bill. "Want to do some driving for me?"

He put his hands up, not accepting the bill. "I'd drive you around for free, Miss Steele. For free. I want to take a beautiful woman to see my beautiful country."

"How about a beautiful place to shop?" I laughed and handed him the address.

"Let me call my replacement. We can go straightaway."

I'd left Mandy in the room, deep in her hacking mode. We could get more done if we split up. I'd given her Eddie's bank login info and she'd run with it, trying to find out where Mrs. Lofton's money went.

Marco returned, driving an old Volkswagen. He was ecstatic to be showing me around and chatted almost nonstop about the history of Rio. His story of the past sucked me in, and before I realized it, we'd circled the main road twice.

I tried to politely butt in, but after five minutes went by and he still hadn't taken a breath, I raised my voice and said, "You're a delightful tour guide, but I really need to get to the address I gave you."

"Ah, right, right, Miss Steele." When he took another look at the address, his face fell. "Are you sure you want to go here? It is bad part of town, the *favelas*. You know this word *favelas*, Miss Steele?"

"The slums. I should be fine—I have you to protect me."

Marco beamed. "I will keep you safe—just stay with me. I was a boxer when I was young and agile." He clenched his fist.

I spotted a Starbucks up on the right and about had a heart attack. "Can we stop, Marco? I need a Starbucks like no other."

"Ah, yes. You American ladies love the Starbucks."

"Yes, we do."

Marco pulled up to park. It was the only American-looking place I'd seen in a mile or so. We were getting away from the tourist part of town and into the real Rio.

"Do you want anything, Marco?"

"No, Miss Steele. I'm not a Starbucks girl." He laughed. "I like my coffee clean and fresh. Starbucks tastes like burnt motor oil."

"We'll have to agree to disagree on that," I said, fairly bursting from the car when he stopped.

The place was packed with locals. I thought I was dressed down in jeans and a T-shirt, but I looked different, very American. This was a problem because I needed to get around without being remembered.

Back in the car, I sipped my black-and-white mocha—they didn't have coconut, much to my annoyance—and Marco looked in the rearview mirror at me.

"What do I look like to you, Marco?"

"Like a pretty American girl."

"That's what I thought."

"We go now, back to hotel, yes?"

I shook my head. "I need to go to this address." I held up my phone again. It was zoomed in on the address printed on the receipt. "Here."

"Yes, but I don't like it. Place is bad. Not a place for a pretty girl like you."

"I thought you were going to protect me, Marco."

Marco sighed. "Okay, but you should be careful. Don't stay long."

I agreed, and he pulled away from the curb. I had to follow my gut, and it said that the only way I would find the blonde girl again was to track her. I had one lead and I was going to take it.

My phone buzzed with a text from Eddie. *I'm at the airport. Goodbye. Thank you for everything. If you need anything in the future, you have my #.*

I texted back. *Likewise.*

*It feels wrong to leave, but I have to. It's too hard to stay when the killers are still on the loose.*

I sighed and then answered, not knowing if it was a lie. *They'll be caught. In the meantime, catch some peace.*

*I will.*

But I knew what it was like to lose a loved one to violence. I knew it would be a long journey before Eddie found any peace.

# CHAPTER 26

THE SIGHTS CHANGED DRASTICALLY the farther we went.

The slums, or *favelas*, were like a town within the main city. Scattered all over in clumps, housing a hundred thousand people to upwards of a quarter million. Shanties, sometimes stacked five high, twisted up the forested hill in what looked like a stack of Legos.

The streets by the hotel had been perfectly swept. Here it was dusty and littered with rank garbage. But it wasn't all bad—music wafted in the air as if it had a life of its own. I'd been told that if I really wanted to learn how to dance, I could learn here. Most parts were safe enough, but other parts were controlled by gangs and drug lords.

Narrow streets made it hard to get around, not to mention the constant pedestrian traffic that crowded the roadway. Marco grumbled, pulled into a short alley, and parked. "The store is up there a block." Getting out, he walked around to my door and opened it for me.

"Wait, aren't you coming with me?" I hoped he would translate if need be.

"No, no, Miss Steele. You leave a car like this in the open for five minutes and the tires and radio will be gone before you return. I stay with the car, Miss Steele. You go do your shopping."

I could protect myself, but the language barrier worried me.

"I will stand here and keep my eye on you. One hour and I come looking for you."

I nodded. "Thanks."

Under Marco's watchful eye, I wandered down the street and looked at each vendor along the way. Fresh fruits and veggies were laid out for sale. Shoes, handbags, and the normal open-market knickknacks were displayed for the casual shopper.

Some of the storefronts were well kept and even had painted windows announcing sales. Others were ransacked and gutted and in need of a good burning.

I avoided talking to anyone and soon found the store I was looking for. MaxxaM & Co. It was one of the nicer ones on the street. I pushed open the door and met a whoosh of air from a hard-working air conditioner.

Racks lined each wall, and benches faced rows of shoes. Mandy would have loved the shoes—all spiky stilettos or strappy platforms. They looked more like torture devices than anything I would want to wear.

I'd blend in a lot better wearing these clothes. I might as well get what I needed. On one of the bottom racks I found wide-soled skater shoes. They were black with pink camo details. Ghastly. But they'd do the trick. Then I flipped through the clothes in the racks until I came to a gray zippered sleeveless hoodie, with "I take what I want" written in silver glitter on the back. After grabbing some skinny black pants with metal studs lining the hem, my outfit was complete.

Then I went up to the register to talk to one of the only people who could identify the Blondes.

# CHAPTER 27

THE LITTLE OLD WOMAN at the cash register reminded me of my grandmother, which brought a bad taste to my mouth. She had silver hair pulled up in a bun and wrinkles so deep her face looked like a carving. I gave her the receipt and asked if she remembered who'd bought the listed items.

"Well, let me see now. I'm not sure I remember who bought what. I do get a lot of people through here everyday."

"She would've been blonde, using a credit card."

"I've travelled all over the world, but this is my home and I ended up here after getting married. Are you married, dear?"

"No, I'm not married." Not even close.

"A sweet girl like you deserves a nice young man."

I wanted to bring her back to the reason I was here. "So, this blonde girl. I really need to find her."

Looking over her glasses at me, the older woman lowered her voice. "I will tell you, dear, that around here you won't get any help. We don't like talking to strangers. Especially about anyone blonde."

I took her meaning, but I wasn't about to let up. "They're killing people."

"Oh, come now. That can't be them—the police are lazy and want to pin it on someone. I haven't seen any blondes come through here. None at all."

I just stared at her. I tried to widen my eyes and look sad.

She glanced up and then back down. Then she spoke as if she were spilling a secret. "The Blondes give back to the people. Sure, they steal. But the money goes to help our schools and orphanages. They're not hurting anyone."

"Yeah, they're modern-day Zorros. Except Zorro never killed innocent women, did he?"

Her eyebrows lowered in confusion. "I'm warning you, if you ask around, you won't get what you want, and you may get a few things you didn't ask for."

I sighed in frustration. "So, you do remember the girl and just won't tell me, or you really can't remember?"

"A little of both, dear."

My only clue was coming to nothing. Looked like buying a loyal crowd was better security than buying the best technology on the market. How would I catch them before they killed again?

# CHAPTER 28

LEAVING THE STORE, I looked down the street for Marco. He was sitting on the back of the car talking on his phone. I texted Mandy and told her this trip was a dead end. I hoped she was getting better results.

I'd only burned thirty minutes. I wanted to walk around a little more and get a feel for the Blondes' territory.

I carried my new clothes in my bag, and because of all the stares I was getting, I wished I'd changed. A flower stall caught my eye and I went up to it. Half the blooms arranged in bouquets I didn't recognize—the supermarket at home never had these. I inhaled the scent of my favorites and asked the vendor their names. With a smile, he gave me a thin little white flower. "It is luck," he said. I put it behind my ear. I'd take all the luck I could get.

"*Obrigado*," I murmured thanks.

Four girls played double Dutch in an apartment alley that smelled like grease and rotting food. Despite the smell, I had to stop and watch. They did twists and flips and moves like I'd never seen. When they saw the small crowd growing, they perked up and put an extra spark into their routine, outdoing themselves. When they finished the song, I clapped. They giggled and nodded, giving each other knuckle bumps.

I wandered deeper down the street, taking in the sights and smells. Most people kept their homes and porches neat and swept, and there was lively conversation from window to window. It didn't look dangerous—it looked like home. Until I heard a low voice behind me. Then all the good feelings were gone.

"*Ei o gatinha*, you lost?" I turned slowly, as if unconcerned, and faced a tall black man. He had a red bandana on his head and a dark sweat-stained V-neck.

"No, just shopping. Do you know where I can find a good set of sandals?" I felt the tiny hairs on my arms stand up and my heart pounded in my ears.

Someone moved behind me and I realized it wasn't just one guy. Three others stepped from where they leaned against a parked car, and at once the street seemed empty. Whoever these men were, they had scared everyone off.

"Yeah, *chefe*, I want me some meat—white meat." All of them were dressed alike. Tough-guy tank tops, shorts, tattoos, and lots of piercings. I should have been scared, but I was just plain pissed.

And, call me suicidal, but I was itching for a fight.

The smallest of the group hissed something I didn't understand and circled me. I took a deep breath. I knew what would happen. I didn't believe I could talk my way out of this, so I had to be smart and quick if I wanted to get out alive.

I slipped one hand around my keychain mace and pressed the other one against the brick wall behind me. I inched toward the main street, trying to put distance between me and the cramped alley.

"Whatever you have, I don't want any."

"Oh, but you do. You just don't know it yet." The leader, Mr. Red Bandanna, took a step forward and the other three fanned out. They blocked the exit. No flight outta here. Time to fight.

I mentally put them each in a danger category. The leader was probably the weakest, physically. His gang did all the work, fought his battles, and therefore he'd lost his touch.

Now the little guy, on the other hand, looked fast and deadly. He had more to prove, and usually he was the one overlooked. I wasn't going to make that mistake. I couldn't make any mistakes.

Mr. Bandanna moved closer and brushed my breast with the back of his hand. I tried not to flinch. "My name is Hector. You want to remember that name because you will be screaming it, begging for more."

I lowered my voice and whispered, "Hector, you should step back."

Hector threw his head back and laughed as if I'd told the best joke he'd ever heard. Then his grin turned into a sneer. He motioned to the two quiet ones who looked so similar they could have been twins. "Take her."

I held up my hand. They paused. "First you must forgive me."

Red Bandanna looked at me quizzically. "For what?"

"For embarrassing you and your little girlfriends in front of God and everyone."

# CHAPTER 29

THE TWINS MOVED IN and I sprang into action. Pulling the
mace from my purse, I sprayed it into the left twin's eyes. He
screeched like a wounded bird and clawed at his face, gagging. I
took advantage of his incapacitation. I nailed him in the balls with
my knee and grabbed his shirt at the same time, spinning away from
the other twin, before dropping him. He fell to the ground. The
smallest guy stood flat-footed and stunned. Lunging toward him,
I emptied the rest of the mace into his face. Rolling the empty can
into my fist, I landed two jabs—then a fist to the throat instead of a
hook. He went down, sucking air.

"You *cachorra*." Hector pulled a knife and pushed the remaining
man toward me. I hastily backed up. With a surprised cry, I tripped over
the guy who was on his back, clutching his throat.

Skidding on the concrete, I scraped my elbows and saw stars. The
twin hauled me to my feet and hit me in the midsection. I couldn't
breathe. Pain shot through my gut and chest.

"You like that? You want it rough, that it, little white girl?" the
twin said.

My vision cleared. The twin was looking over his shoulder at

Hector and held me up by my shirt. Bringing my knee up, I racked him again. When he doubled over, I smashed my knee into his face. Blood poured from his nose and he fell over, gurgling and cursing.

Stumbling backward, I managed to regain my balance and run. Each step hurt. My eyes were burning and lungs gasping from the mace floating in the air.

Hector's heavy footsteps chased after me, cursing and promising what he'd do to me. Didn't sound like he was offering a foot massage and pedicure, so I kept running. I thought I was heading in the direction of the car, but I might have gotten turned around. Marco was parked just down the street. Or was he one block over to the left? I couldn't get my bearings.

Left it was. Dodging a trash can, I almost twisted my ankle. The alley I chose was a dead end … so much for my good female intuition. It smelled like feces and rotting cheese, not a pleasant combo.

A sense of irony hit me. Not too long ago, I was the one chasing someone else into a blind alley. There was nothing I could do—no doors, nothing to fight back with. Even my purse was back somewhere between here and where three guys sucked wind.

Boots grated on the ground and a deep, guttural laugh echoed off the walls. Hector stood at the mouth of the alley. He had a pipe in his hand about the size of a baseball bat. Now I was scared.

He walked slowly toward me. "This is the fun part."

My fear brought out something in me that liked to fight. The dark monster that lurked, just waiting for someone dumb enough to come close to its cage. And I was dumb enough to voice it.

I glared at him "Fun for me. By the time I get done with you, you'll be breathing out your belly button."

Growling, Hector rushed at me with the pipe raised. He was muscular, but he wasn't fast or flexible. I think those were the only two things I had to my advantage. Swinging at my head, he grunted and I ducked. The pipe slammed into the wall. Hector cursed. I tried to get around him, but he blocked me. He was faster than I'd anticipated.

My head seemed to clear, as if the fog of fear was vanishing, and in its place was the same feeling I felt when I baited and killed Williams. Hector was no different. A part of me wanted to kill him ... and not just to survive. "That all you got, little boy?"

Twisting the pipe around, he clipped my shoulder and I went down face-first. My hands took the brunt of it and I rolled instinctually. The pipe hit the concrete where my head had been a millisecond before— that was a killing blow. He was in a rage.

Grabbing a broken crate, I blocked his next blow and kicked him in the knee. I heard it snap and he cried out. But that was like a spear poked in a bull's side, slowing him down but enraging him further. He raised his foot to kick me—I saw my opening. Jerking my knee up, I swept his leg out from under him. It didn't knock him off his feet, but it unbalanced him. He staggered back, opening up his chest area. Now was my chance to hit his throat. I pulled the crate back.

But before my blow landed, I heard a hollow thud. Hector hit his knees. I watched as his face smashed into the ground and blood burst from his lips and nose. He was not even a foot away from me, so close that I could smell his sweat and the iron in his blood.

I didn't move away, didn't look up—just stared at him. He was out cold and would have one epic headache in the morning. I watched the blood stream down his head and the bruise pool under his skin.

"Sarah." Solomon's voice ripped me from my trance. He held his gun—he must've used it to pistol-whip Hector.

I lifted my eyes to meet his. "Solomon?"

He helped me to my feet and wrapped me in a hug.

"Are you okay? Did he hurt you?" He held me at arms' length and looked me up and down. I touched my forehead, where a bruise was forming. He hugged me again, and I went limp in his arms.

"I'm okay," I said, my voice shaking. "Just had to say hi to some of the locals."

His eyes lit up, and then he yelled. "What were you thinking?"

# CHAPTER 30

SOLOMON MARCHED DOWN THE alley and I followed in silence. A few people started coming out of storefronts and shanties. My purse and sack of clothes lay on the ground and I picked them up. They appeared to be intact with all my stuff still inside.

"I have a car waiting. Marco will take me back to the hotel," I said.

Solomon didn't turn around or even acknowledge that I'd said anything. We walked back to the main street and I saw Marco standing by the car with a worried look on his face. Next to his car was a dark blue SUV.

Solomon walked ahead of me, but turned now and again to make sure I was behind him. My whole body was starting to tremble, and my throat clenched so bad it hurt.

Marco waved when he saw me, and I waved back. His smile turned to a concerned stare when he saw my disheveled appearance.

"Miss Steele, what happened to you?"

Solomon stuck out his hand and flashed his badge. "FBI. Miss Steele was in an altercation. I need to bring her in to get a formal statement. I'll take it from here."

Marco stared at Solomon and then shook his head. "I promised I would drive her back to her hotel …"

"No need. I will drop Miss Steele off after we get her statement."
Solomon opened the passenger door and I got in. I nodded to Marco
and he grumbled something and got in his car. If I'd been in complete
control of my voice, I would've said something reassuring to him, but I
was too shaken up.

Solomon got in and started the engine. He didn't look at me,
wouldn't say anything. I got that he was upset because I, well, I guess
I'd lied. But I didn't need him knocking heads when I was fully capable
of knocking heads myself.

But then I also realized how completely thankful I was that he
showed up when he did.

# CHAPTER 31

WE WERE OUT OF the slums and heading back to the hotel. The line Solomon gave about taking my statement was just so he could drive me. My hands were shaking. It wasn't often that I craved alcohol, but I could really use a drink. Now.

Solomon gritted his teeth and then jerked the wheel to the right, pulling off the road into a small lot next to a surf shop.

"We agreed that you'd stay out of this. That you'd let me do my job."

"I know, but—"

"But what? This isn't Boise. You can't go walking around here alone. Most of all in the slums."

I swallowed, trying to make my voice sound tough. "Not sure you noticed, but three of the four guys who jumped me were on the ground when you showed up. I know it's not Boise. What *you* need to know is that I'm an adult, I can do whatever I want, and I had a lead."

"A lead? That wasn't *your* lead. That was *our* lead. You gave us the purse—we know that the Blondes shopped at the shoe shop. What do you think this is, some game where you play Nancy Drew and get the bad guy? This gang is out killing people, Sarah, and the point is that you lied to me."

"You're one to talk," I said, then fell silent.

He cleared his throat. "You could've been killed out there today. If you had a lead, you should've called me. If you want to help, do it by filling me in, not going around me." Solomon turned in his seat and I could see something in his eyes. It wasn't anger—that was all over his face, but not in his eyes. What was it? Was he afraid for me? He swallowed. "I don't want to think about what could've happened to you today."

I stared out the window and tried to be somewhere else, not wanting to acknowledge the warmth I felt at his care. "Just take me back. You don't have the right to care anymore—you're just some guy I went out with a few times." I regretted it as soon as I said it.

I looked at him from the corner of my eye and saw hurt flash in his eyes. "Some guy?" He cursed and slammed the SUV in gear.

I think I just broke up with Solomon. For the second time.

# CHAPTER 32

THE ELEVATOR DOOR OPENED and I marched down the hall to my room. Solomon followed me—why, I don't know. Probably to lock me in. I felt like I was seventeen again, sent to my room for sneaking out.

I pushed in the key card and it turned red. I tried again—nothing. My hands were still shaking from the assault. Muttering a curse, I tried once more and the little light finally turned green. I pushed into my room, turned, and started closing the door to keep Solomon from coming in.

"Sarah—"

"Just leave me alone." He had his body half in the room and half out. He slipped in without much effort.

"Don't act like this has anything to do with me, or this case, or even you lying to me. You're mad about something—"

"Dang it, Solomon, quit analyzing me."

He turned away, and my eyes started burning.

I turned him back around and pushed him against the door. Heat flooded my system and I was kissing him. He kissed me back and I pinned his arms against the door.

I had never kissed him like this—most of the time, our kisses were tender. This was forceful and aggressive. It made my head swim and my body burn with desire. It certainly wasn't unpleasant.

"Why do you like fighting in dark alleys?" Spinning me around, he pushed me onto the downy bed.

"Yeah, and you like playing the knight in shining armor."

Solomon loosened his collar and tossed his suit jacket. How he could wear a suit in this humidity was beyond me.

"I can't believe you said I was just *some guy*. You push every button I have."

I sat up and grabbed him. Pulling him on top of me, I kissed him. His lips anticipated everything I wanted. He put one hand beside my head and the other he wrapped around my waist, pulling me to him. I gripped his shoulders, my heart racing and my breath caught in my throat.

I wanted to forget everything and just lose myself in him. Be in his world, by his side. Yet I knew I couldn't get any closer to him. How could I feel something so strong for someone I hardly knew?

I couldn't let myself do this.

With a gasping breath, I pulled away. "Easy, tiger." I propped myself up on my elbows and tried to keep my tone playful. He kissed me on the cheek and stood. Once again, he didn't push me.

"I have to go. The local police will have the four men who attacked you in custody by now. I called it in and I can go ID them so you don't have to. I'll get your statement later."

"Okay. Besides a statement, do you need anything else from me?"

Solomon winked. "I need you." Stepping closer, he moved his hand to my waist and kissed me softly. No matter what my brain was telling me to do or the hurt inside screaming for me to back away, I couldn't. The fact was, I didn't want to.

"Now. You will stay here, won't you?" He put on his suit coat.

"I don't think you intended that to be a question, did you?"

"No, but I won't treat you like a child. That was wrong of me. Can you and Mandy just promise me you'll let me know if you're going into something dangerous?"

"Sure. Speaking of Mandy, where is that girl?"

# CHAPTER 33

MANDY TOOK ME TO a nice, quiet beachside restaurant. It was a luau-style place with the pig and all. I was very tired—all the emotions of the day and the street fight had drained me completely. I craved a good, comforting meal and then a long sleep.

"If not for the kidnappings, murder, and gangs of rapists around here, this could be a great place to vacation." Mandy grinned like a dork and I laughed in spite of myself.

"Yeah, yeah. We have only two days left here—the time has flown by. So what'd you find out with all your hacking?"

"I think I may have found something, but I need to follow a few more threads. Let's not talk about it tonight—you and I need a break." She took a bite of coconut rice. "So, you and Solomon. Spill it."

"What? Nothing. I mean … something."

"Uh-oh."

I wanted to avoid this conversation, but only because I didn't know what to make of it all. Solomon was not the mouth-breather Neanderthal type. He seemed mature and like he was living up to his potential, which was really all I could ask for. "Why can't things ever be easy?"

"Because this is how life goes. Life isn't fair. Things go wrong, people do bad things, and I gain weight when I sit around all day eating Bunny Tracks. Sarah, you are making this hard for yourself."

"No, I'm not. I want to be happy, to be loved, but …"

"But what? No one knows who you are. You keep it all hidden and it takes a really persistent person, like myself, to dig under that hard shell and see you, the *real* you. And you haven't told me anything about your past. Not really. You *can* be happy, but I'm not sure you really *want* to. And I think it has to do with all your secrets."

She was right. I hated when she was right.

"Why bring out your cattle prod all of a sudden?"

Her mouth quirked up. "I think you really like Solomon. You haven't ever had a guy who can keep up with you like he has." She shook her spoon at me. "And I don't want to see you mess it up. So I'm trying to get to the bottom of your psychosis, which, of course, means digging into your past."

Biting my lip, I tried my hardest not to fight her. I had a past I didn't want to think about. I had buried it deep, thinking it would stay buried. "You know about my mom, how she's in prison for life?"

Mandy nodded.

"I don't ever talk about it because no one knows the real story, and I'm scared that if anyone finds out, it will—" My throat closed, and I could barely say the words. It had been so long.

"What, Sarah? Do you think you'll lose Solomon or me?" She reached across the table and took my hand.

"No, I'm scared that I'll lose me."

I was scared that I already had.

# CHAPTER 34

MANDY ORDERED COCONUT ICE cream and we moved to a private area on the beach. There was a large, round bed to lounge on, and our ice cream came a few minutes later.

"Now this is more like it. Ocean breeze, the sun setting on a cool bed, eating your favorite ice cream." Mandy was trying to lighten the mood and it was working.

"The food is amazing. Not to mention being here with my best friend." I took a bite of ice cream and decided I should get it all out. "There is something, Mandy, something that happened after my mom went away. Today reminded me of it."

She looked out to sea, giving me room to tell the story.

It was now or never. "I first went to stay with my aunt, and I was with her until she died of lung cancer. Somehow I thought it was my fault, not the four packs a day she sucked on. If it hadn't been for a nice Sunday School teacher, I probably would have lost all hope then. I was ten years old and without any family to speak of, so I was put into foster care.

"Mr. and Mrs. White were my first. They were the good ones. But she got pregnant and they didn't keep me long. Then I landed with some bad ones. It took eight homes before I landed with the Gibsons. They were amazing people and I was so lucky to be raised by them."

"And they died in a car crash. Sarah, I'm sorry."

"Nineteen. I was nineteen. You'd already moved to California to go to college. So once again I was alone, no real family and going off to college by myself. I met this older student, Andy. He was so sexy and kind of a bad boy. No, not kinda. He really *was* a bad boy. I liked him almost immediately."

"I don't remember you talking about him."

"I never talk about him, to anyone." I sighed. "We went out three times before he hit me. It was a slap. He was drunk, and I thought it was my fault because I'd spilled my drink on his jacket. I knew a lot of girls who were abused by men and I never understood why they stayed, why they didn't just leave or have the guys arrested. But once it happened to me, I understood. It's like this weird connection happened in my brain. When he raged at me, I took that as love. If he could feel so much, get so worked up over something I did, that was a form of passion."

I gripped my spoon so hard it bent. Dropping it in the ice cream, I paused and took a shaky breath.

"That doesn't seem like you," Mandy said. "I mean, if a guy ever hit me, I'd want to kill him. Leave, do whatever it took to put him away, but not think it was love."

"I know, Mandy, it was twisted. I was seeing something and my mind was telling me lies about it. This went on for a few months when something clicked. I saw what I was doing, what I was letting happen. And I finally realized it was wrong. So one night when he came to my apartment drunk and in a rage, I fought back. I was already doing a lot of kickboxing, so I was in really good shape. He hit me and I fell. I always kept a baseball bat by the door for protection—I know, imagine that—so I swung it and broke his knee. He hit the floor so hard

I thought I killed him."

"Dang," she whispered. The compassion on her face soothed me.

"Yeah, well, I had some pent-up hostility. I beat him pretty bad. Broke four ribs, his arm, and leg. After he passed out, I dragged him to my car and drove him to this old park where all the druggies hung out. I waited for him to wake up. Then I put a knife to his balls and told him if I saw him again I would kill him. Never heard from him again."

Mandy stared out at the beach and I could tell she was processing it all. She also had a look of righteous anger on her face, and this was the side of her that made me feel safe—when she got defensive on my behalf. I'd never been more thankful for her.

I took a slow bite of ice cream. "You know, it's kind of like what's happening with this case. Everyone sees a twisted view of it. The poor want the Blondes to be heroes, so they see them that way. The rich want to see the Blondes as evil criminals. Even Eddie and Tanya's story might be twisted in a way I don't see."

Mandy thought for a moment and then said, "We all twist things to see them our way. It's how we cope. And I think you see things clearer than most. At least, now you do. You're a lot different than who you were. You seem like you want to find out who you are, and you're really strong. If I can help, I hope you know I'm here for you. Always. Even if you are a crazy bat-wielding psycho girl."

"Hey," I said, but couldn't help the smile that peeked through my frown. "Everyone's a head case. You just gotta decide if they're a head case worth putting up with."

"I guess you're worth putting up with a bit longer. Since you're so exciting."

"Speaking of exciting, are you mad we wasted tonight and didn't get to check anything off your list?"

Mandy took her notebook from her purse. "Naw, see here …" She wrote in her scrawling handwriting: *Have a heartfelt talk about Sarah's past.* Then she checked it off. "There. We've been so productive tonight."

# CHAPTER 35

BLENDING IN WOULD BE harder now that over half the tourists were gone. A few days ago, the private beach was so packed that at times it was hard to find a spot to lay out. Now it looked like a ghost town.

We were in our room. Mandy sat on her bed cross-legged, typing on her laptop.

I was thinking about how I could get more information from the slums without asking strangers. I needed to talk to someone who heard all the news and wasn't known for keeping their mouth shut. I knew just the place. "Want to go get our nails done? I also want to dye my hair so I don't stand out so much."

Mandy looked up from her laptop and gave me a flat stare. "So nearly getting raped and having a huge fight with your sort-of exboyfriend wasn't enough to keep you from dropping this thing?"

I put my hands on my hips and glared at her. "What do you think I am? A pushover? You're still on board, aren't you?"

She shrugged. "Well, yeah, but I didn't get attacked. I'm all safe behind this here computer."

"So are you coming with me or hiding out here?"

"Fine, I'll go. I'm keeping my hair just the way it is, but I need to get my nails painted with palm trees so they'll match my new suit."

"There's nothing more satisfying in life than matching your nails with your outfit … Sounds like something Mother Teresa would say." She threw a bag of Sour Patch Kids at me.

Glaring at me with her signature "I'm pretending to be mad at you" stare, Mandy shut down her laptop and dug in her bag.

She changed into a dark blue sundress and I tore open the package of candy and found a green one. I loved Sour Patch Kids—well, any candy, really—but the sour ones held a special place in my heart. I popped another green one in my mouth. "We should rent motorcycles while we're out."

A huge grin spread across Mandy's face. "Brilliant."

She slipped off her dress.

"No. What are you doing?" I tapped my watch. "Let's go already. It's like I've spent half this vacation waiting for you."

"I gotta look the part." She made a rocker face with her tongue out, which I couldn't help but laugh at, and then she changed into jeans and a black tank top. She put on a black collar necklace and bemoaned the fact that she didn't bring her steel-toed boots. After she put on smoky eye shadow and dark red lipstick, I raised my eyebrows, impressed.

"From girly to Goth in thirty seconds."

"What this outfit really needs is my dragon bracelet," she said with a sigh.

It was true. The bracelet was the missing link to the outfit. "Tell you what—when we get back, I'll snoop through that bellhop's locker."

"Really?"

"Really."

After Mandy was ready and I was out of green candy, we took the elevator to the lobby.

Marco wasn't on duty, but I got the other valet to tell me the closest place to rent some motorcycles. He told me the address with a smirk, which I wondered about … until we arrived at the shop three blocks away.

It was a scooter shop. Cute little scooters lined the lot in all kinds of pastel colors: blue, purple, pink, and green—it was like the Easter bunny had decorated them.

"He sent us here on purpose. We've been punked," Mandy said, looking sorely out of place. After we checked with the salesman and he told us that the nearest motorcycle rental was ten miles away, we just had to accept our fate.

"Let's do it."

"Over my dead body," Mandy argued. "I've got a reputation to uphold."

I motioned around us. "It's not like paparazzi will snap a photo of you on a pink scooter."

She narrowed her eyes. "How do you know?"

I laughed. "Come on, Mandy. It'll be like we're fourteen again. And your list didn't specify which type of 'cycle.'"

"I didn't mean this type of 'cycle,' for sure." But then her lips spread into a grin. "I'll do it, but only if you ride the pink one."

I wrinkled my nose.

"And I get to put a picture of it online."

I groaned, pretending it would be torture for me, and then readily accepted. I was never very excited about big motorcycles—their power scared me, although I never let Mandy and Rick know. My view of danger was rather enigmatic. I loved taking risk in some areas, but liked most things simple and safe.

After we signed the leases and got our keys, we picked helmets. I got a Hello Kitty one, just to complete my look. Mandy snapped a picture of me in it, and then she chose a purple sparkly one.

The gentle purr of the scooter felt good. It felt safe. As we pulled

148 | AARON PATTERSON

onto the road, Mandy shouted, "I need to tell you what I found out on the money hunt."

"Spill it," I said, eager to hear the details.

"Later. Fun vacation scooters, nails, and your new hairdo—then work crap."

"Lead the way, scooter butt."

Suddenly, a car swerved right in front of us. We slammed on our brakes, narrowly missing the bumper. Mandy exchanged a colorful repartee with the driver, which made my ears turn red, and then the car sped away.

This would either be a lot of fun, or we would both die.

# CHAPTER 36

VITORIA ADJUSTED HER REARVIEW mirror and continued through the light, past the Bank of America building. She'd been to Chicago three times in the last fifteen months. She hated going to the States. They reeked of pride and arrogance.

She turned into a parking garage and found a spot on the third floor. The garage stank of rubber and urine. She'd heard American tourists claim that Rio smelled bad. Well, that was like the zebra calling the jaguar spotted, or whatever the old saying was. She took the elevator to the ground floor and walked up two blocks, her head down to keep from having to look at the morons who infested this city.

Checking her cell for the time, Vitoria cursed and picked up her pace. She was a few minutes late, and they didn't like it when she was late. Last month, she had some conference call and it took forever to get the landline set up. They had said no cell phones and they were starting to get pushy. This could become a problem if they expected her to be the fall guy.

"Morning, Miss …?" The guard sitting behind a desk in the lobby smiled and looked from her to a chart.

"Beth Young. I have a meeting in Suite 3201."

The dark-skinned man with a Celtic tattoo peeping out of his shirt rubbed his brow and typed on his laptop. "Uh, yes, there you are. Can you sign in for me, please?" He pushed a clipboard forward and Vitoria signed in. She had to stop herself before she wrote her real name.

"Thanks, Miss Young. You can go up—elevators are to the right." He smiled and motioned toward a bank of three elevators.

"Thank you."

Vitoria took the middle elevator to the 31st floor and found suite 3101. It was different every time. Sometimes they met out of the city; other times it was in a high-rise like this one. It drove her nuts.

She took a breath and opened the door. The small office was sparsely decorated with landscape paintings and cheap fake plants with dusty leaves. There were two chairs against one wall and a door leading into what she imagined was a conference room. The door was open.

"Glad you could join us." Mr. Grant stood and buttoned his suit jacket. His gut pushed against the poor jacket and it was a wonder the button held up.

She didn't care to give a reason why she was late. It was none of their business, and who were they to give her a guilt trip?

Grant cleared his throat and motioned toward a blonde woman sitting on the far side of the table. "This is Susan Moore. She is handling distribution. And you know Gil Manchester." He nodded to a wiry man with a scar under his eye and teeth stained with cigarette tar. He stood and stuck out his hand, staring at her chest. Vitoria took his hand and tried not to cringe.

Gil Manchester was her main contact and she didn't mind him so much over the phone, but in person he put out the rapist vibe.

"Vicki, so good to see you again."

Was that the new nickname he'd made up for her? "Gil." She pursed her lips and wouldn't give him the satisfaction of conversation.

Grant poured water into a glass from a crystal pitcher and handed it to her. Then he shuffled a few papers and sat down. "Let's get to it. First thing we need to go over is the status update on the shipments to the States. Port to port, what have we got?"

Susan Moore handed a report to each of them. "Our deadlines have basically been derailed. Baltimore was on schedule until yesterday when they hit a few problems. I'm not sure if they're on schedule anymore."

Grant grunted. "Figures. Our people over there are high half the time. Any way to get around them, or get the shipment in by train?"

"No, we need the port. We have some people on it, but it could take some time to get our goods processed. As you can see from the report, we are short across the board. We need more supplies and we need to get our permits through." Her voice rose and Grant held up his hand.

"The permits are not your department. Let corporate handle that."

"I would if they would get them through the city. We're behind by six months here in Chicago, and that's just here."

"I said it's not your department. Get the shipments in and keep out of the rest."

Susan relented and sat back in her chair, red in the face. Seeing her so mad was almost comical.

Taking a sip from his glass, Grant sighed and pushed the report away. "Moving on. How are things on your end?" He looked at Vitoria, and she smiled.

"Right on target. Give me three months and I'll have the whole business wrapped up so tight they'll be able to kiss their own elbows. And the cash I pull in will even out Miss Susan's obvious deficits."

Susan glared. Gil chuckled and Grant acted unimpressed. "You have two months. Keep doing what you're doing, and then our moderator will step in and start handling business. You'll be under him just as long as it takes to get him caught up."

Vitoria seethed inside. Being under a man was exactly what she was escaping—she thought this job would give her that independence. At least it would be the last time she'd be beneath one. "And then you'll get our passports and visas and get my team out of Rio. You'll do everything you promised." Even though it was a statement, not a question, Grant answered.

"Of course."

She scanned his face, looking for a trace of dishonesty. Usually something in their tone or behind the eyes let her know when people were lying. He had none of that. So why did she feel like he wasn't telling the truth? Vitoria felt surrounded by the enemy. She couldn't wait to get out of here, to the airport, and back home by the next day.

But they had a few more things to cover first. She leaned back in her chair with a sigh and bided her time. One day she'd be in control. And it'd all be worth it.

# CHAPTER 37

WE FOUND A NICE day spa called La Pushe and Mandy picked a manicure-pedicure package. She went into a different part of the spa and I followed a thin guy with a fro so big, I had to sneak a picture with my phone.

"Right this way. Do you like this chair here?"

"It's fine." I sat down and he spun the chair so I faced the mirror.

"Now, now, my blonde beauty, what are we doing to you? A splash of red? A strand of white? Maybe go crazy and cut it all off—it is very modern for a beautiful woman to shave her head."

I cringed. "Oh, no, nothing like that. I was thinking of going dark."

He furrowed his brow and shook his head. "You girls always want what you don't have. The blondes want to be brunettes and the brunettes want to be blondes."

"Yeah, we're never happy." I winked at him and he grinned.

He took my hand and ran his finger up my arm. "You know, you could pull it off. Maybe not dark black, but a blue-black, yes." He shook out a shawl and placed it around my shoulders, where it settled around me like a blanket. Leaning me back, he washed my hair and massaged my scalp. I couldn't have kept my eyes open if I'd tried. It was so relaxing. But the hairdresser wasn't having any of it. He wanted to be best friends.

"What's your name, buttercup?"

"I'm Sarah Steele. What's yours?"

"Reggi, just Reggi. Now, do you want to have some curl to match your new color?"

I thought about it for a moment. "Why not?"

Reggi was a talker, and I soon found out he'd grown up in the slums. He learned English from his aunt, who was a teacher. "She told me it would get me out of the slums, and she was right. I love being a hairdresser. Don't tell anyone, but I bought into this here spa—half owner now." I bet he told everyone that.

"That's smart. So if you're on your way to the big times, why are you still doing hair?"

He puffed out his lips and muttered, "Oh, girl, I love this stuff, and if I was stuck back in the office, I wouldn't get to talk to lovelies like you, now would I?"

I closed my eyes and relaxed as he combed my hair and started on the dye job. We chatted about this and that, what we liked to do in Rio, the clubs to go to and the ones to avoid, and I tried not to sound like a tourist. I carefully formulated my next question. I'd appeal to his flair for the dramatic—which I'd noticed he had in plenty.

My lip trembled and my face closed in mock pain. I took a shuddering breath, squeezing one lonely tear from the corner of my eye.

"Why, buttercup? What's the matter?" He was all concern.

I sniffed. "It's nothing."

"It's never nothing that makes someone cry." He turned my chair around and took my hands. "I'm not touching your hair again until you tell me. Out with it. What's the matter?"

I hid my face in my hands for a few tense seconds and then

whispered, "The Blondes."

Reggi cocked his head in confusion.

"I want them … no, I need them."

He was really confused at this point. "You need them, honey?"

I pressed my hand to my heart. Okay, maybe that was too much. "It's my friend—Mandy—the one I came in with. The doctors just told her she has cancer."

Reggi gasped. My lip trembled and I nodded.

"She looked so healthy," he exclaimed.

"Her cancer is spreading fast," I said. "The thing is, she doesn't have enough money for the treatment. I don't either." This is when I laid it on thick. "And…" dramatic pause, "we're both orphans and have been taking care of each other our whole lives. I can't imagine a day without her." I covered my mouth with my hand.

"But what does that have to do with the Blondes?" Reggi asked.

"If only I could contact them and ask for some money for her treatment." I took a hiccup-breath and dabbed at my eyes. "I know they give money to orphanages and churches—they could save her life."

"Of course, buttercup. They'd do that in a heartbeat, I know. Especially Emilia."

Hope lit up in me at the mention of a name. "You know them?"

"No, no—uh, I don't know them personally."

"Where can I reach Emilia? Can I leave her a note … anything?"

He stood up and rocked back on his heels, thinking. He turned me back around and started on my hair again. Frowning, I let another tear slip down my face.

Biting my lip, I asked, "Is it because they're changing? I mean, it's not like them to kill."

He lowered his voice and leaned in. "Look, Sarah, their leader is getting crazy. I mean, off-the-rails crazy. They were just girls out having fun and making some money, but she's the one doing the killing."

"I promise I won't—"

Reggi interrupted. "If I help you, what are you gonna do?" He ran a comb through my hair, which was now dark black with a hint of blue. "I want to help you, but I have to trust you."

"I'll just leave her a note. I don't even have to see them or anything."

His face closed in thought.

"Reggi, if Emilia is a good one, she could save my friend's life."

He blow-dried my hair in silence for what seemed like an hour. I didn't want to say anything. I learned a long time ago from working with witnesses that once I asked for a commitment, I should shut up. Whoever talked first lost.

Finally, he shut off the blow dryer. "I'll give you an address—not for Emilia, but for someone who can reach her. You can drop the letter off there. Don't go inside or talk to anyone or even knock on the door, understand?"

I stood up and threw my arms around him. "Thanks, Reggi."

He grunted and turned me toward the mirror. "There, you look even more beautiful than before. Dark hair suits you."

I did look good. My hair was styled with part of it piled high in a messy bun and the rest curled just past my shoulders. "You're a magician."

Mandy walked up to us, and Reggi rushed to her and nearly started crying. "I'm so sorry to hear about your health … such a lovely girl… so young. Stay brave, okay? We'll get you some help."

Her jaw dropped and she looked to me in shock. "Act sick," I mouthed.

She instantly drooped, putting her hand on her head. "It's kind people like you who make me want to keep up the fight. Bless you for your kindness." She kissed him on the cheek. "Bless you."

I gave her a thumbs-up. Mandy really was the best friend a girl could ask for.

Now I had a decision to make. Should I take the address straight to the FBI, or should I do this on my own?

# CHAPTER 38

"THAT WAS FUN. LOOK." She held out her hands and I cooed over her polished nails, which had a garish palm tree painted on each one.

"You look like an official tourist now, but I'm glad you had fun. I got a lot done."

"Only *you* would say that after going to the salon." Mandy eyed me as I climbed on my scooter. "So what did you get? You have that look again, like you just kissed a boy or robbed a bank."

"I have an address." I waved a piece of paper and grinned.

"Whose address?"

"Oh, just an associate of one of the Blondes."

"You're like a magnet for this stuff. You sure you don't want to open up our own private investigator agency? We could solve, like, three cases a day with your ability to dredge up information."

"But I like my job, and I like having money to buy food and pay bills and go to movies and stuff. Now tell me your findings. We had our fun and you promised."

Mandy put on her helmet. "I tracked down all the places where Mrs. Lofton's credit cards were used and put together a list. I bet one of the stores has a security camera. And if we're real lucky, we can get a look at one or more of our blonde friends."

I whistled. "Good job, Mandy. Where to first?"

"What do you mean? Your address is a way better lead—we should go there."

"I want to find a face for one of the Blondes first. And then I want to take it and the address to Solomon." As soon as I said it, I knew it was the right decision, the wise one. After all my dark musings about what I'd do if I caught the Blondes, I knew I shouldn't meet one face-to-face.

Mandy agreed and I texted Solomon to meet us for dinner. I looked at my watch. "Well, it's a long time to wait for him. Let's run your leads."

"You know it—don't mess with Idaho girls." Mandy started up her scooter.

I snapped a picture of her and texted it to Rick before she could stop me. She'd probably be more embarrassed by that picture than if I'd snapped one with her next to a male stripper.

# CHAPTER 39

WE DROVE ALL OVER town from one end to the other. I was
sweating so much that the front of my shirt was soaked—not
an attractive accent to my outfit. Sitting on a scooter was more
exhausting than it should've been—perhaps because of the stress
of driving through traffic. The other vehicles seemed like they
purposely aimed to run us over.

After a bus turned into our lane, forcing us onto the sidewalk,
I screamed at Mandy over the road noise, "We're using the metro
tomorrow."

We were striking out big time. Most of the stores didn't have
cameras, or they didn't have a clear shot of the Blondes. Or so they
said.

We pulled into a gas station to fill up and Mandy stretched. "This is
not going as well as I hoped. The last one is a motorcycle dealership. If
we strike out there, we're up a creek."

I was so glad I had GPS on my phone—getting around would be
a nightmare otherwise. We would take the metro tomorrow if we went
anywhere, but I was glad we'd tried the scooter thing today. Seeing the
city from the street level made me feel more connected, mainly because

my life was flashing before my eyes every three seconds.

After buying some junk food to settle our nerves, we followed my GPS to a large dealership. Bikes of all sizes and shapes took up the oversized lot.

As we rode in, a few salesmen looked at us as if we had just defiled their temple with our scooters. Mandy was blushing to the roots of her red hair, and I felt a twinge of compassion for her bruised pride. She usually rode a badass Deus Grievous Angel, which she and Rick had saved up years to buy.

"I hope they don't kill us and burn our scooters," I said. "I don't think our insurance will cover it."

"I don't care if they kill us," Mandy said morosely. "We deserve it." And then her eyes lit on a motorcycle. "Hey, look. Is that a Street Tracker?" Her embarrassment forgotten, she went to pore over the bike's engine.

After I dragged her away from it, we went into the office. "I'll take front man on this, okay?" I whispered, and she nodded.

The air conditioning hit me hard, making me shiver. A tall black man with a huge smile held out his hand and I shook it.

"Welcome. I see you girls like to ride." I wasn't sure if he was making fun or not, but under the circumstances, I assumed he was.

"I'm a casual rider, but Mandy here likes all kinds."

"You have a nice selection," Mandy said.

"We do. We are the largest dealership in Rio. May I ask, if you two aren't looking to buy, what brings you in today?"

I cleared my throat. "We're working for the FBI as consultants on a case concerning the Blondes and the murder of Mrs. Lofton." Out of the corner of my eye, I saw Mandy grit her teeth. Oops. I should have warned her about our cover.

The tall man put his hands on his hips and his smile faded. "I'm not sure what we have to do with that."

But Mandy was nothing if not flexible, and she jumped in. "We followed one of the stolen credit cards here. It seems that one of the gang members used it to buy a bike." Mandy pulled out her phone, punched a few buttons, and said, "It was last week. Let me get you the date and time."

"Do you have security cameras?" I asked.

"We do. We have four on the lot and three inside. As you can see, we have a lot of property to protect."

"Could we take a look at the tapes?" I crossed my fingers, hoping this man was not a Blonde sympathizer.

"I would need to see some kind of ID. I can't give out information like that."

My anger began to boil. I was hot, sweaty and tired. "Look, you can deal with us or you can deal with the FBI and the police. Do you want the police all over this place, scaring your paying customers, taking official statements, making you go in for questioning?" I took out my phone and pretended to put in a number. "I can call them right now, have them force you to give up your tapes …" I looked up. "Or you can let us see them—no hassle, no mess."

He held up his hands. "No, no, don't call." He took a long breath and looked around. "Truth is, the manager isn't here. I'm in charge, and he would kill me if he knew I was talking to you. You can look at the tapes, but you can't take any of them—just look." He rubbed his hands together nervously. "And if you see anything in the tapes that would be of interest to the police besides the Blondes …"

Mandy smiled coyly. "We won't say a thing."

# CHAPTER 40

IT TOOK THIRTY MINUTES to find the right tape. Mandy kept our nervous salesman busy as I watched the videos. I fast-forwarded to the time of the sale and watched two blonde women walk up to the register. Both kept their heads down as if they knew where the camera was.

"Dang it." Just as I was about to give up on getting the money shot, one looked up, exposing a clear view of her face. She had smooth brown skin, a mouth that looked comfortable in the frown position, a cute little-girl nose, and empty black eyes. They made the deal quickly and left.

Turning, I gave Mandy a look. She got the hint and asked if he sold any Harleys. "Sure, I'll show you." They both left the small back room. I backed up the tape and paused it right when the blonde woman was looking up. I took a picture with my phone, fast-forwarded the tape, and left the room.

We thanked the salesman and hustled out of there before his boss came back.

"What'd you get? Did you see anything?"

I took out my phone and showed her. "Looks like we have our first picture of one of the Blondes."

# CHAPTER 41

WE WENT BACK TO the hotel to shower and change before dinner with Solomon. I also needed to keep my promise to Mandy about looking for her bracelet, which she reminded me about every five minutes or so.

Putting on a plain, button-up white shirt, black pants, and tennis shoes, I followed one of the bellhops down to the basement. I tried to look all business, and I griped with him about the lack of tourists as we rode the elevator down.

The place was buzzing with laundry bins, rows of warehouse racks full of cleaning products and supplies, and about two dozen staff hard at work while the managers barked orders. Everyone spoke English, even down here, as it was required at the hotel.

I quickly found the women's locker room. Just as I slipped in, I sneezed. Then I leaned against the wall and put my head in my hands. Stumbling forward, I "accidentally" brushed a woman's shoulder.

"Oh, so sorry," I said. Then I sneezed again for dramatic effect.

She took a step back. "You not feeling well?"

I shook my head miserably. "I'm so sick and I really need to slip a note to my sister, who's working. But she won't answer her cell, of course, and I need to know what locker she's in. I wouldn't even go to the trouble except I'm watching her kids, and I can't leave them alone with my cousin for long …"

"Don't worry, honey. I will help you."

I was always a bit surprised when people were eager to help. I wished I were as open to the world. Holding back a sneeze, I said through a stuffed nose, "Her name is Lucy."

For a second, the woman narrowed her eyes. "I didn't know Lucy had kids."

"Maybe because I'm the one who takes care of them all the time."

Her eyes lit with understanding. "Yeah, Lucy seems the wild type, not exactly one to sit at home with toddlers. She's always rushing from one adventure to the next with that husband of hers. That's her locker." She pointed. "227U."

"Thank you very much. You saved me so much trouble."

"Feel better soon, okay? Drink lots of fluids and orange juice."

Her kind, motherly advice almost made me feel bad for being such a total liar. I gave her a smile. She watched me walk to the locker, and I slipped a blank piece of paper from my pocket through the opening at the top.

I sighed with relief when I heard her leave the locker room. Only a few women were showering in the back, so I had the place mostly to myself.

The lock had a three-digit combination. Easy peasy. Most people only twirl the first number after they lock it and don't worry about changing the rest. It'd take one out of nine tries. On the fourth try, the lock popped open.

The locker was neat. It had an expensive mountain trekking backpack, and … ah. Her bruises suddenly made sense. There was a paragliding shoulder harness hanging on one of the hooks. That would definitely cause some bruising, even on the smoothest of trips.

I dutifully went through the rest of her bag, but no dragon bracelet showed up. Looked like Mandy was wrong. Our vision of things could get so screwed up—we see what we want to see. Because this girl was a bellhop, we thought she was in need of our compassion. Instead, she was happily engaged in a hobby.

Guess I'd just have to tell Mandy her bracelet was gone for good. I frowned. I hated being the bearer of bad news.

# CHAPTER 42

WHEN WE WALKED INTO the restaurant, my eyes caught on Solomon's figure in a polo shirt and khakis. He looked like he was about to play a round. Mandy's eyes caught on something else. She clasped her hands together as if she were in a fairy princess movie and then pointed.

A huge macaw, as big as my forearm, with bright green feathers and a gorgeous red chest, was sitting on a perch on the hostess's table. "Oh my God," she breathed. "He's beautiful."

"He's beautiful," came the bird-voice reply. It eyed her with interest. "Polly got a cracker?"

Mandy gasped and surged forward. The bird took a few cautious steps back on the perch and I laughed.

"If you say 'Mandy,' I'll give you all the crackers in the world."

The parrot nodded its head up and down. "Sandy."

"No, *Mandy*."

"Candy," the bird repeated.

"Mannnn-deeeee," she annunciated loudly.

"Dandy."

Mandy exchanged a glance with me. "Okay, now it's just messing with me."

I laughed. "I'll leave you to your bird-talk. I'm going to Solomon."
I left her repeating her name, her nose two inches from the bird's face.

As I made my way across the room, I checked out the restaurant,
wondering if Solomon had any backup or partners around. The place
was almost empty—an elderly couple crooned sweet nothings in
each other's ears at a booth, five young men laughed and drank more
than their share at the bar, and a family of four sat at a table beside
Solomon's, sharing a bucket of shrimp. I guess he came alone.

Before I sat down, I knew Solomon was angry, but he tried to hide
it by not looking at me. What did he have to be mad about? Brazil was
a free country too. I knew he wanted me to stay out of all this, but now
it was in my blood. I had to see it through. Or maybe he was angry that
I'd dyed my hair. It was a toss-up.

After I gave him the information I'd gathered from Reggi and the
bike shop, I looked away as if I didn't care whether he took it or left it.

He spoke grudgingly. "As much as I hate the fact that you two
played detectives, I think I can use what you gave me."

"If by that you mean 'thank you' and 'I'm super impressed at your
skills,' then you're welcome."

He took a big gulp of his red wine. "Right place, right time?"

I held back a smile. "It's a gift."

Mandy's voice was getting louder and louder. I wondered for a
second if I should intervene, for the bird's sake, but then decided I
shouldn't spoil her fun.

The waiter came and took my order—a white sangria and a tall
glass of water, no ice. I'd heard that some restaurants made ice with
unfiltered tap water. "So what's next?"

He replied without thinking. "I think we should get the locals in
on this. They may know the blonde woman by sight. She probably
wouldn't be in any of our systems. And I'm sure they'll have

information on the address you got."

I raised my eyebrows. "You think they'll do a sting, maybe go in with guns blazing?"

"No, I don't think so," Solomon said, not realizing I was joking. "We need to find out who lives there first. With the picture and the address, I think we have a good shot at bringing them all in. I'll tell Eddie it was thanks to you."

I couldn't help but feel proud. And a bit more partial to Solomon than I had realized. Maybe we would never be close, but this—sharing a meal and talking about evidence—this was fun.

Solomon took a bite out of his rockfish and I followed the movement of his jaw. When he glanced up, I quickly looked away.

"I like your hair. It looks good dark."

I smiled and looked down at my fork. "Thanks."

"Did you hear about the three bodies they found today?" Solomon asked.

I put my hand to my mouth. "No."

He took a sip of his red wine. "Yeah, three women. They found each of them in their cars, all were robbed, and the Blondes used their credit cards and checks. It looks like they're not even kidnapping them anymore—just killing them and leaving."

I wondered if the crazy leader had turned her followers into murderers. Of course, they didn't see it as evil. Everyone is the hero of her own story. Not the sidekick or antagonist or mentor or minion. The hero.

Someone had to stop these heroes.

"Something has definitely changed. With serial killers, there's an evolution that takes place, and it seems like a similar pattern is going on." Solomon stared out the window as if lost in thought. "Every murder is the same—with a gun, at close range. The leader is taking over, forcing his or her agenda on the group."

"Or she's converting them."

It was like they wanted to scare the public, to show they could do anything and kill anyone at any time. They were spreading terror—losing Rio its tourist business. But why, to what end? And did it have to do with just one psycho, or was it bigger than that?

I wished I could go behind the lines, into their place, and see what they were saying. The police and FBI had a subjective view—they could only see it from an official perspective. I wondered if my view was real—untwisted.

"What are we going to do?" I asked.

Solomon took a breath and looked right at me. "We're going to find them and do whatever is necessary to stop this insanity."

We were distracted by a shriek of happiness from Mandy. She kissed the bird on the nose and called over, "It said my name. I think it really likes me, too."

"Man-dee," came a squawk. Mandy fed it a cracker. Then she took out her notebook and marked that line off her list of to-dos.

# CHAPTER 43

ONCE SOLOMON AND I had finished eating, we left Mandy
to polish off her dessert and went outside to walk along a short
boardwalk. The sun was setting in a glorious array of orange and
pink and other fantastic colors I couldn't name, and for a few
minutes we just stood in companionable silence, enjoying the view.

Then Solomon attempted to hold my hand and the good feeling
was gone. I crossed my arms and said, "I'd like to see this through to
the end. Let me go with you to the police."

He tried to tell me that it would be better if he went to the police
alone. Something about how they would want to know why I was
getting involved in a police matter, and he didn't have an answer for
them other than that I was a nosy citizen.

On a whim, half-joking, I said, "Just tell them I'm a freelance
contractor for the FBI. You guys hire them for different things, don't
you?"

He paused. And then, as if he had been thinking it all along, he
said, "Okay. It might be smart to make it official, though. This case is
getting big, and if we go to trial, we could lose on a technicality. But
having an attorney on contract would be helpful. I'll tell the office at

home to send the necessary paperwork."

I froze, not believing what I was hearing. Did he actually just say I could work for the FBI? My mind whirled, processing the info. Perhaps he'd wanted this all along and had been waiting for the right moment. I brushed that thought away but didn't dismiss it entirely. He was, after all, FBI.

Then he said something that made my blood turn cold in my veins. "I know you have secrets, Sarah, and I don't need to know them all." His big brown eyes widened and he spoke earnestly. "I know about the evidence at your mother's trial and the mismatched dates that made the judge throw out the case."

I wanted to run so badly, but I couldn't move. I heard myself say, "What dates?"

His voice turned gentle. "Your father was walking dead long before he received the blow to the head." I swallowed. Tears came to my eyes and I hated myself for them. "He was being poisoned. Your mother wasn't the only one involved, as she was gone on a trip during one of the doses, so she had help."

I turned my back to him, unwilling to let him see any kind of weakness that might be playing on my face. It was one of my greatest fears—hearing my father's death brought up by a law enforcer.

"I—I—"

He brushed a stray hair off my neck. "That's ancient history. It involves you, so I was interested, but I promise on my own mother's grave that I'll never bring it up again unless you do."

I had a good BS detector, and I could tell he wasn't lying. I believed him. Was I stupid?

"Why did you tell me that?" I asked in a rough voice, then cleared my throat.

"Just so you'll know you can trust me to keep a secret and not ask questions."

Those were the two best qualities I thought anyone could possess. My shoulders sagged and I leaned my head against his chest. My cheek rubbed his soft shirt, and I closed my eyes.

His voice returned to all business "So, you working on contract for the FBI. Whaddya think?"

This idea was complicated; a lot of risk would be involved for me. Even though my faith in Solomon was rising, it was still too much to decide so spur of the moment. "I'll have to think about it."

"Text me your answer by eight o'clock," he said, turning away.

Eight o'clock. Ugh. There went another chance to sleep in.

# CHAPTER 44

SOLOMON AND I MET up for breakfast in the lobby café while Mandy got ready. Before my coffee had even arrived, Solomon set a stack of papers in front of me.

"They've already sent the contract."

I narrowed my eyes. Maybe he'd had it with him the entire time. Was I being set up?

He continued, leaning over my shoulder to go through the papers. "I had someone go by this morning to print them off."

He riffled through the papers until he got to the last page, where a line had been highlighted as if I were a second grader who needed to know where to write my name. Did he really think that would work? I always tried it on clients I wanted to hurry through the process.

"It'll take me all morning to look through this—"

He interrupted with a cough-laugh. "Oh, yeah … you're a lawyer."

"Which means I'll analyze these papers inside out and upside down."

He turned his face. We were so close—almost cheek to cheek. He smelled like mint, coffee, and faintly of sea water.

"Did you go swimming this morning?" I asked.

"Yes. I can't pass up an ocean swim."

"And you don't sleep very well," I surmised.

His eyes roved over my face, taking me in. A longing in his expression drew me in. Without a thought, I leaned in and kissed him. Our lips barely touched, but it sent warmth through my body. Then he pressed his lips gently against mine, moving his tongue into my mouth, and before I knew it I'd grabbed his neck and pulled him closer to me.

"A-hem."

We broke apart to see Mandy standing there with raised eyebrows as if she'd just caught us making out during church.

Solomon put on his sunglasses and I poured sugar in my coffee. Mandy just looked at me as if thinking, "I can't leave you alone for one minute."

Tipping his head Mandy's way, Solomon said, "While you study your papers, I'll talk to your witness. What was his name…?"

"You can't talk to him. He gave *me* the address and I don't want to bring him in on this. Can't you tell the FBI that a confidential informant gave the address to you? Or that it was me? All part of the service I provide as a freelance contractor."

"*Potential* freelance contractor. Or you could sign the papers right now and we could go down to—"

"Not on your life," I said in a flat tone.

"Okay, then. I hate to do this, but I'll fudge the dates so you're covered for all last week."

It was hard to draw the line when it came to the law. I used to be a down-to-the-letter girl, but in the past year I had found myself more concerned with justice than following every rule. Was it wrong? Maybe, but sometimes two wrongs do make a right.

# CHAPTER 45

I SAT ON A lounge chair on our patio. Poring over the papers with a skeptical eye, I didn't find any words undefined or anything I couldn't agree to. I even called Joshua a couple times to confirm things.

Mandy had gone out shopping, and by the time she was done, I had signed my name with a flourish at the bottom.

"You may now call me Special Agent Steele," I said as she lugged her pile of bags into the room.

"That has a nice ring to it," she said. "Hey, look, since you've been so busy catching criminals, I went ahead and bought you an entire wardrobe."

My eyes widened in shock as she pulled out shirt after shirt and dress pants and skirts and leggings and even a couple pairs of shoes. I was even more surprised to find that I liked them. I smiled when she pulled out a T-shirt that said, "Another day went by and I didn't use algebra."

"Good friends can order meals for each other," I said. "But only truly great friends can pick out a wardrobe for you."

"And lookee this." She pulled out neon-green bikinis that looked like they glowed in the dark. "No matter what you say, we're going out in these tonight."

"After all this shopping you did for me, I'll do anything you tell me." Feeling an overwhelming affection for her, I gave her a big hug. "Thank you."

She squeezed me back, then handed me an outfit. "Put this on. You'll look the part of secret agent."

"Yes, ma'am." The matte black tuxedo pants were a perfect fit, as was the mint-green blouse with a mock collar.

"Are you meeting Solomon now?"

"Yeah." I paused. "I have a bad feeling about all this. How things will finish with the Blondes, I mean."

Her eyebrows creased. "Things like this never end well."

"No, I mean, I feel like we're missing something. Things don't add up. Why would they kidnap people for over two years and one day just start killing?"

"Who knows? Maybe they figured it was easier with no one alive to ID them." She took out a small compact and began retouching her makeup.

"It's more than that—it has to be. The other thing is Eddie Lofton …"

"What about him?"

"I don't know—just got a hunch. Do me a favor. Look into all the murdered women's financial situations. If they were married, see if you can find anything out of order."

Mandy hopped up on the edge of the desk. "You mean beyond the stolen credit cards?"

"Yes, everything. It feels like when they started killing, they also went from picking random people to specific targets. So far seven women have been killed, including Mrs. Lofton. See if they're tied to anyone important. They were assaulted—they could have been tortured for information, passwords, usernames, bank accounts. The police haven't released the names of the three most recent victims, but they should soon."

"I bet Solomon knows. I could get their names and run a background check on them, see what I can find."

"Sorry to leave you again," I said before heading out the door. "I know this—"

"Shut it," she said, engrossed in her laptop. "We've got work to do."

# CHAPTER 46

I RODE TO THE police station with Solomon. We parked in a small lot in front of a faded yellow two-story building. It was in need of repair and a paint job, but so were most buildings in this part of town. Solomon had called ahead and we had a meeting with the police chief and the lead investigator in ten minutes.

A large man in a uniform and glasses met us and offered us coffee. It smelled like dirt water, so I declined, but Solomon took a cup. Once again, I had to question his taste.

"This is Chief Lucas." Inspector Paulo waved his fat finger toward an even fatter man in a white button-up shirt with a tie that was much too short. "Chief, this is the FBI—Mr. Solomon and his consultant."

"Nice to meet you." Solomon stuck out his hand and the chief shook it. He eyed me with open suspicion.

The chief didn't stand up, merely leaned over his desk. I decided to lay low on this one. The vibe in the room was that a woman should not be in this line of work, and it was not the time to fight for my rights.

"I am very interested in what you have to say about our little problem."

Solomon nodded and took a seat in a chair next to mine. The

cramped office was cluttered with boxes, files strewn here and there, and crooked pictures of girls in bikinis on the walls.

"I emailed you our report so you should have everything we have, but I wanted to go over it with you personally. The last thing the FBI wants to do is step on your toes."

Paulo cleared his throat and scooted his chair forward a little. The three of us were on the other end of the desk—it felt like a meeting with the school principal. "I looked over this report—you have some good intel here. What do you know of this woman?" He held up the picture off the security camera.

"In the course of her investigation," Solomon motioned to me, "Miss Steele had a run-in with this woman after the murder of Tanya Lofton. Sarah works with the FBI as a freelance consultant and we brought her on this case because of her special skill set."

Chief Lucas wiped his forehead with the back of his hand and looked at me. "What special skills?"

I decided to go in soft. "I have a knack for finding people and making them talk. Call it a gift."

"Miss Steele is also a criminal lawyer back in the States and a very good investigator."

The room fell quiet and both men looked me over as if I was the newest animal at the zoo. Chief Lucas finally spoke, and I let out my breath. "Very well." Motioning to Paulo, the chief cleared his throat. "What did you find out about the girl?"

Shifting in his seat, Paulo glanced through the file and back up to the chief. "We got lucky, a much-needed break. One of my people recognized the girl. We confirmed her to be Emilia Lopes." He handed us all a file on Emilia. "She's been in and out of juvie on drug possession charges. We don't know where she's living, and the address doesn't match anyone in relation to her."

"What *do* we know about the address?" Chief Lucas asked.

Solomon took out a piece of paper and handed it to Lucas. "We discreetly asked around and found out that the house is owned by an elderly woman by the name of Margret Caio. She has two children— one daughter, and a son who died a few years ago in a local gang war. Not sure of her connection to Emilia or even if there is one. We're going in somewhat blind."

"We'll send a man down there to talk to Caio, see what she knows," Chief Lucas said.

Paulo mumbled something and the chief shot him an irritated look. "Speak your mind, Paulo. What's wrong?"

"We've been trying to get this gang for a long time. Up till now we've had nothing—no leads, no pictures or anything to give us a hint of who the girls are. Now we have a name, a face, and an address. We can't blow this. I think going in as police would be a mistake. You know how everyone feels about the Blondes on that side of town."

Solomon agreed. "Maybe go in undercover, see if we can get her talking before we take the hardline approach."

The chief pushed back in his chair and licked his lips. The buttons on his shirt strained under the pressure of his girth, and I was prepared for one to pop off and fly across the room.

"For once, I agree with you. It should be handled differently."

Paulo looked straight at me. "Miss Steele, you blend right in. You should go talk to her. We could put a wire on you and see if you're as good as the FBI claims."

Solomon stood up as if a bee had stung him. "No, I'll do it. Sarah isn't trained for this kind of thing."

Chief Lucas snorted. "You reek of America. And a few minutes ago you said Steele is one of the best. Didn't you hire her to do this sort of thing? She goes in with a wire, she has backup. It's not a dangerous situation. Our people will be on it. You can assist, but this is my show now."

Solomon's face flushed and his jaw worked.

I stood up and put a hand on his shoulder. "I'll be fine. I know her face; if Emilia is there, I'm the best person to talk to her. And if only Margret is there, you know that I'm more likely to get an old woman to talk than you are."

After a respectful nod to the police, Solomon turned and left the office without a word. I let him go. This wasn't his call. I held back a smile at the thought of going undercover. The rush was the same as when I was in the courtroom—the challenge of getting someone to break and give up something they wanted to hide. I was good at getting people to talk, and now all my skills would be put to the test.

I was ready for it. Time to see if I was right about the Blondes.

# CHAPTER 47

"IT'LL BE FINE. I bet she's one of the girls' grandmothers or aunt or relative. Or maybe their crack dealer," I winked.

He took me in his arms and whispered in my ear, "I don't like this, Sarah. It feels wrong."

"Well, if it's any consolation, I would have gone to talk to her alone if I wasn't trying to keep you in the loop. What's the worst that can happen? She'll jump me and I'll have to fight off a senior citizen?"

"Not funny."

"I'll be careful."

"You better." He kissed my cheek and all at once I wanted him so badly I ached. I leaned in for a kiss just as he pulled away.

He was so confusing. He was the one who wanted me on his team, and now he was acting all prickly. He was getting to me, and I wondered if I was getting to him in the same way. I knew he liked me, but to what end?

What was I doing, thinking about our relationship at a time like this? I'd better start doing what I did best—catching the bad guys. Or in this case, the bad girls.

I was dropped off a few blocks away from Margret Ciao's house.

Trash littered the small road, but the shady palm trees lining the sidewalk made it cool and comfortable. The houses weren't nice by a long shot, but they weren't shacks, either.

Paulo and two other officers were in a small, unmarked car around the corner. Solomon was on the street, dressed like a homeless wanderer. He didn't have access to the wire feed, so he'd be the eyes. I suspected he was there just to be close to me in case anything happened.

I started knocking on doors a block away from her house. I pretended to be a missionary trying to raise money for a children's shelter. The police had some flyers made up and I handed them out to seem legit, just in case she was a peep-out-the-window kind of woman.

Almost everyone I talked to gave me something. I promised myself I'd get the money in the right hands. Their generosity humbled me because everyone who gave me money looked as if they could really use it themselves.

I was soon at the rickety door of Margret Caio's small house. The door's glass window was broken and covered with black paper. I knocked and then quickly stopped. The door shuddered on the hinges, and I feared I might take it down if I knocked again.

An old lady swung the door wide open. A threadbare floral muumuu hung around her fragile body, cinched with a leather woven belt that looked handmade, and she wore black leather boots that didn't really complement the outfit. Her face was caked with foundation and green eye shadow was smeared over her eyelids. She looked up at me and a smile cracked her face.

I smiled back. "Hello, I'm with the West End Children's Shelter. I was wondering if I could talk to you about what we're doing to help out the local homeless children." I tried to use my sweetest voice without sounding too cheesy.

She looked at me over the top of her glasses, and her hand shook a little as she took the flyer. She had the whitest hair I'd ever seen. It was pulled back in a French braid.

"Come in, dear. Standing in the door is bad luck." I relaxed my stance and stepped inside. "Do you look after children with no families, or all homeless ones you find?" Her English was good. I didn't even hear an accent.

"We accept kids who are orphaned and also teens having trouble with the law—drugs and gangs."

Her expression turned wistful, as if thinking of a happy memory. "We've been having so much trouble with gangs lately. Sit down, dear." She shuffled to a small kitchen and I sat down on an uncomfortable wool sofa that smelled like Lysol. Every inch of the wall was covered in framed cross-stitch. From the traditional "Home Sweet Home" sampler, to intricate landscapes, to Betty Boop, to quotes from the Bible. It was like a museum for cross-stitchers.

"Tea?" she called from the kitchen.

"Yes, please." I started to relax and scanned the room for pictures or some clue to the connection she had with the Blondes. I suddenly felt a bit overwhelmed. Reggi might have lied and this could all be a wild goose chase. And if it was, I would have a lot of people none too happy with me.

"Here you go, dear." Margret handed me a small teacup. "Now, tell me about this program you're working with. Or you can just tell me the real reason you're here."

My pulse kicked up a notch. She was a sharp cookie. "It's Margret, right?" I took a big sip of tea. It was sweet—too sweet—but I gulped it down.

She nodded.

"I'm here because I ran into someone you may know, and I was worried about her. Do you know a girl named Emilia Lopes?"

"Are you with the police? You're American—what do you want

with Emilia?"

"No, I'm here as a friend, nothing more. She's in trouble."

The old lady smiled. I shifted in my seat.

"Serious trouble. I need to talk to her. I want to help."

Margret took a lump of sugar from a small glass dish on the coffee table and put it in her tea. "Ah, yes. We love it when Americans help us. Oh, wait—" She shot me a pert look. "We're both Americans, aren't we?"

What should I say to that? The way her eyes were lit up and always smiling, while her body language was tense, made me feel strange. Did she want to help?

She continued. "I was her teacher in the sixth grade. Taught all of them before they got mixed up in that gang."

"The Blondes?"

"Yes." She raised her chin.

Why was she, out of everyone, admitting to knowing them? She must have something on top of me—I just couldn't see it. Her ease and confidence set me on the edge of my seat. I eyed the door. It wouldn't take much force for me to barge out of here if I needed to. But until she made a move, I'd listen and get as much information as I could. She appeared to love talking.

"Emilia's a good kid, but scared. Scared people do bad things."

Something thumped in the next room. I turned just as the door opened and the girl from the motorcycle security camera stepped in. Margret set her teacup down.

I stood, but my legs wobbled. What was happening? The ground shook under me and my ankles gave way. I fell to the ground, scraping my hip against the coffee table. Although my mind was still sharp, my eyelids grew heavy and they closed before I could stop them. It was as if my body had completely shut down while my mind remained alert. A perfect nightmare.

I heard Margret get up and stand over me. "Two things you should know about this place," she said. "One, never drink anything you didn't see poured in front of you. Two, in the slums we live together, we die together, and we're willing to take a bullet—or even kill someone—for one of ours."

"I'll get her off your hands, Avó. I'll take her—"

Margret's voice was harsh. "Shush, shush. She can hear everything. She's just paralyzed."

I knew what was about to happen. Internally, I braced myself. Emilia brought a gun butt down on the top of my head. Darkness descended and I tried to fight against it, but I couldn't move. Then something metal knocked against my head. Searing pain filled my thoughts, and then … nothing.

# CHAPTER 48

MY HEAD POUNDED. ROUGH cloth was pulled over my face. Blended colors and lights filtered through the bag or blindfold, but nothing clear. I was in the trunk of a vehicle, with my hands tied behind me. The car smelled like vinegar-based cleaner and baking soda. It had an acrid tang of metal.

Then I remembered the hit on the head. How long had I been out? I would have one big-time migraine in the morning. It felt like a beast in my skull was trying to claw itself out.

The vehicle turned and the road got bumpy, and I smelled the unmistakable odor of dry dirt. I breathed in dust through my nose and sneezed. My hands were bound behind me with what felt like zip ties and my mouth was gagged. I was in pain, sweating, and tied up. So yeah, I was in one heckuva tight spot, to put it lightly.

We stopped after what felt like a few more miles, but I didn't know because I couldn't tell how fast we were going. A door opened and closed and I felt the dark side of me start to move. It was like a calm fog rolling through me, and I let it take over.

Heels clicked on pavement, moving away from the car. This was my chance.

First, I tried the backseat. Kicking off my shoes, I examined the back of the trunk, feeling nothing but smooth plastic. Hauling back, I kicked it. The thud reverberated through the little space. It was a solid box—no outlet to the backseat. I cursed whoever built this model.

Next, I tried the weak spot—the lock. Slipping my shoes back on, I kicked the middle of the trunk lid over and over again with both feet. My face felt hot and sweat poured down my back. Someone banged on the lid of the trunk and I stopped.

The trunk opened. Someone grabbed my shoulder and heaved me up. I didn't fight—my feet were free and I wanted them to stay that way.

"Get up, and don't try anything funny." She spoke in a low voice, as if to sound tough. Was that Emilia?

A moment later, whatever covered my head was yanked off. I blinked in the sunlight and saw Emilia. She took my arm and guided me toward the warehouse.

My hands were still tied behind me, but at least I could see. I still had the wire on me, so I wasn't afraid for my life. This would go one way or another, but I knew I had what it took to come out all right. At least, that was the pep talk I gave myself as she walked me toward a large old structure.

I didn't see any other buildings around, and only two cars were parked on the side lot. The place looked nondescript. I could see how useful it'd be as a hideout—there was a quick exit to the freeway, and quick escape routes in almost every other direction. If trouble came, they could split, fast.

Emilia whispered forcefully at my side. "You had to keep pushing. Why didn't you just leave me alone?"

The girl's eyes were erratic and scared. Why was she so scared? She was the one with the gun tucked in the back of her jeans.

"Look, I can help you. Just talk to me. Let me go and we'll talk to the FBI. I can get you a deal. You don't have to do this."

She turned and shook her head. "You don't get it, do you? You can't help me. No one can beat her."

# CHAPTER 49

THE FEELING OF BEING in total control, though on the outside it seemed like I was the one in danger, reminded me of when I was waiting for Williams. It was addicting. This darkness I felt was like a drug, making me see, smell, and hear things better.

Emilia took me inside, past an open area filled with crates and boxes. Hundreds of them were stacked, with long roller tables for sorting. It was a packing and shipping area.

In the corner was a small office and I spotted a few rooms to the right   maybe bedrooms or a bathroom. A tiny blonde girl came out from one of the rooms and stared at me. She wore high heels and was dressed like one of the Real Housewives of L.A. I was looking at one of the Blondes.

"Emilia, what are you doing? Who is *she*?"

Emilia pulled me closer as if I was some sort of prize she didn't want to hand over. "Vitoria found her snooping and asking questions. I guess she found Avó."

The small woman rushed into the office in the far corner and Emilia pushed me into a chair. "Stay put and keep quiet."

I nodded, then went still. Carefully, when Emilia wasn't looking,

I noted all the exits. And waited. I should have been scared, but I felt calm and ready for whatever was about to happen.

A door slammed and three women rushed around the corner. I pegged the tallest one as the leader, Vitoria. She wore black cargo pants and a tank top. She was very pretty, but her eyes looked dead, as if she were one of those replica dolls—they looked real, but had no spirit.

"Vitoria, what are you thinking?" a dark-skinned girl asked. "Who is this and why did you bring her here?" She looked like the most athletic and militant out of them all.

Emilia shrank back and stood next to me.

Vitoria took out a cigarette holder. She opened it with a click, calmly tapped one out, snapped her lighter, and drew in a deep lungful of smoke. Her crew shifted, uncomfortable. I knew what she was doing. She was changing the atmosphere—making it hers, not theirs.

"This snowflake was at *Avó's* house asking questions. She knows who Emilia is. I think she's a cop or something. *Avó* said we should kill her."

The skin on my arms tingled with excitement.

Vitoria smoked as the other two girls watched, standing a few feet behind their leader. No matter what this gang had started as—a sisterhood or a way out—it had obviously developed into a one-girl show. Except for the dark-skinned one, these girls looked anxious and afraid. Afraid of Vitoria.

Vitoria finished her smoke and threw it on the ground, then pressed it with her boot. "How would she know who you are, Emilia? Did you do something? Something stupid?"

Emilia looked at the ground. The small blonde behind Vitoria cleared her throat. "She went back to the hotel to give the husband his wife's necklace. She got chased by some woman—I'm guessing this is her."

Emilia gasped. "Lili, you promised." Her voice cracked and I knew this would get ugly fast.

Lili shrugged and looked down at her feet. Emilia, on the verge of tears, bit her lower lip to keep from crying. I wanted to help her—I knew that much. I just didn't think I could say anything in her favor, so I kept quiet. The next time we were alone, I'd use all my wiles and convince her to leave with me. She had to. I had a bad feeling about her lifespan if she stayed with these chicks.

Vitoria turned to Lili. "Check outside—make sure we weren't followed. Mia, check the American slut for a wire."

Lili ran to the front door and disappeared outside and Mia walked toward me. My heart began to pound. I had a small wire running around my ribcage and up my bra. If she checked my shirt, she would see it. My former excitement turned to fear for the first time.

I knew it was a risk, but I was dead no matter what. I had to stall and let the people on the other end know it was going down… now. "We know who you are. I'm Sarah Steele, FBI."

Vitoria moved past Mia and tore my shirt open. Buttons ripped off and scattered across the floor. Gasping, Emilia took a step back and Vitoria grabbed the small wire and yanked it hard. I winced as the cord stung my skin when it broke free.

Lili walked back in the door and shook her head. Vitoria gave her a nod and held the broken wire in front of Emilia's face.

"You stupid little brat." I didn't even see the gun. One second, Vitoria had the wire in her hand, and the next, she had a Glock pressed to Emilia's forehead. The report made my ears ring—someone screamed. Blood sprayed my face. Emilia's head snapped back and she went down.

# CHAPTER 50

LILI WAS CRYING AND yelling at Vitoria. She held Emilia and
rocked back and forth, cursing through her tears. Vitoria spit at me
and then turned and walked back to the office. My head pounded. I
had to do something and do it fast. If she would kill one of her own,
I had no chance of survival.

Mia paced and tried to get Lili to stop crying, but nothing was
working. Mia opened a can of beer from the fridge and held it to her
forehead. "It's her own fault." She took a gulp of the beer. "She was
always the weakest one."

Lili groaned. She tried to wipe blood from her hands, but it was all
over her. I wriggled my hands, trying to free them, but the bonds were
too tight.

"She's dead, Lili. It's over. You need to calm down." Mia tried to
pull her from Emilia's body, but Lili punched at Mia.

"You did this. You ratted on her and now she's dead," Mia said.

I had to convince Lili to leave. And take me with her. "You'll all be
dead if you don't get out of here soon. Cops are already on their way."

Mia stepped back and looked at me as if remembering I was there
for the first time. Her face registered fear. "How much time do we

have?"

"Ten minutes, maybe less." I had no way of knowing, and as far as I knew, Solomon and the police had no idea where I was. "I can help you and Lili. Things don't have to get worse. You don't have to end up like Emilia."

Mia looked down at Lili and the dead body of her friend. "Vitoria will take care of us—she always has."

"Like she took care of Emilia? The police know your names; they're interviewing your families as we speak. They're moving in. Nowhere will be safe. They know what you look like. This is over, Mia. The best I can do is get you off easier for helping me."

Lili sobbed and muttered something, but I didn't understand what she was saying. I twisted my hands in the ropes, but couldn't get them to loosen. I could get up and run, but with my hands tied, *all* I could do was run.

Why did I let them put a wire on me? I should have done this alone. The police, the FBI, Solomon—they made things more complicated. I knew in my gut that I should never have trusted the police and the whole wire thing. Every criminal moron on the planet knew to check for a wire.

"How?" Lili asked.

I was getting through to her. I didn't know if it was the bloody body in her arms or the realization that the police were coming. "If you help me take Vitoria in, they'll let you off because you helped capture her." I knew it was a lie, but this was not the time to be a saint. Not when these girls' lives were on the line.

Lili seemed to consider this, but before she could make up her mind, Vitoria came out of her office, gun drawn. "What are you doing, Lili? Kill her."

That was my exit line. Launching to my feet, I ran as fast as I could. My shoulders jerked back and forth, as it was awkward sprinting with my hands behind my back. A gun sounded and I heard something scream by my ear.

# CHAPTER 51

I DODGED BEHIND A row of crates and kept running toward the back of the building. Their footsteps sounded behind me. I wondered if it was just Vitoria or if Mia was coming after me too.

A shot rang out, and wood splintered the spot where my head had been a second before. I twisted left and saw a door at the end of a long hall. It didn't look like it could hold up to much pressure, so I put my shoulder down and crashed through, falling in a mess of legs and broken wood.

Rolling, I arched my back and pushed myself up. Having my hands tied would get me killed.

I found myself facing a long canal and a dock. It was some sort of inlet. Farther down, it opened up to the sea. Other than some tall grass, there was nowhere to hide. Running around the building looking for an exit wouldn't work, as there was a fence on each end. And even with my athletic abilities, I couldn't climb a fence with no hands.

My lungs burned and I tried to calm my breathing. Two options: outrunning Vitoria, or hiding in the water from her. Since Vitoria had numerous vehicles to choose from, swimming would be the lesser of two evils. I ran down the dock and jumped over the side. The cold water shocked my system. I went all the way under. Struggling, I kicked my legs and broke the surface. I caught a glimpse of Vitoria clearing the broken door.

Sinking under again, I analyzed my choices. If Vitoria didn't kill me, I would drown. I had to get my hands out of these ropes, or at least in front of me.

Hunching over, I pulled my arms under my feet, but couldn't get them around. My shoulders burned with the strain—I needed air. Tucking up my legs, I forced my hands down and felt my left shoulder slip out of its socket.

Blinding pain shot down my arm. But I used the extra space, got my legs through the hoop my arms made, and kicked to the surface. Even though my lungs were on fire, I managed to gulp air quietly. I pressed my arms to a wooden dock support post and wrapped my legs around it, keeping just under the overhang.

Vitoria ran to the end of the dock and looked out toward the ocean. Her shadow darkened the water.

She screamed a curse. "Steele, don't try to hide from me—this is not a game. You have no idea what you're involved in." She moved slowly back up the dock, getting closer to where I hid.

"You think this is some small-time gang kidnapping women for a few credit cards? You think this is just me and my girls? They'll come for you."

My mind raced and my shoulder ground bone on bone with each breath I took. Vitoria stopped and listened. I knew she would find me—the sound of my breathing was so loud in my ears.

She stomped her foot like a spoiled girl.

Her voice rose. "I'll kill you slow, Steele, cut off each finger and force feed you them one by one. Then I'll cut off your eyelids and make you watch the rest. You think you'll live? There's nowhere to go. You can't swim all tied up, so if you're hiding in the grass, I'll find you.

Give up now and I'll make it fast."

Sounded like I wouldn't be invited to her slumber party.

Just when I thought I would get away free and clear, Vitoria looked down and laughed. I stared into the dark pools of her eyes. I sucked air and pushed myself under the water, but it was too late.

# CHAPTER 52

VITORIA DROPPED TO HER knees, looking down into the water and holding the Glock out, ready to shoot. If I could see her, she could see me.

My feet hit the muddy bottom. I bent my legs and pushed as hard as I could, launching myself up and out of the water. I looped my hands over Vitoria's neck. I fought through the pain grinding through my shoulder. Her face slammed into the dock, but she didn't fall into the water. I hooked my leg over the dock edge and hauled myself up. I still had my arms around her neck, so I took advantage of the momentum and wrapped her in a chokehold from behind.

Vitoria gagged and thrashed under me. I twisted my legs through hers, forcing her flat on her stomach. She was strong, and she curled her legs under and flipped onto her back just as a gun fired.

Vitoria screamed—her body stiffened. I snapped my head around to see Mia standing at the water's edge, holding a gun. She ran forward and kicked me hard in the ribs. I felt one crunch. I gasped, and the pain was so intense I couldn't breathe.

Mia was talking, but all I heard was my own inner monster growling at me.

*Move, get away, and find the gun. Don't think, just act, or you will die. Let go and live.*

Squirming out from under Vitoria, I scrambled sideways, trying to get away. Another shot echoed over the water and I felt something sting my neck.

I looked down the dock, but couldn't find Vitoria's gun. Rolling to my knees just as another shot rang out, I saw the Glock lodged under Vitoria's leg. She was on her back, coughing and gagging.

"You're not the leader anymore, Vit. I'm gonna run the show now, right after I take care of this American."

Mia was on the other side of Vitoria, holding a silver gun. It was trained on me. I looked her right in the eye and winked. Her face registered shock and it gave me the second I needed. I dove for the Glock, grabbed it with both hands, and fired.

Two blooms spread across the front of her shirt. Mia hung in the air for what seemed like an eternity. Her hands went limp and the gun slipped from her fingers. Her knees buckled—she hit the dock hard.

I stuck the Glock to Vitoria's temple. "Move and I put you in the ground." Time seemed to slow down. She twisted away and backhanded the gun from my hands and into the water. Dang, she was fast. Blood seeped from her side—she couldn't run. We both got to our feet at the same time and I managed a low sidekick to her right hip. She fell to one knee.

My body was overheating from adrenaline and pain, letting me know that I had a shoulder out, broken ribs, and had been shot. I pushed through the pain. This was not the time to nurse a wound.

Mia's silver gun lay just within Vitoria's reach. She went for it. I kicked again and this time her arm snapped, bending the wrong way. I heard yelling and the sound of boots pounding down the dock.

My hand wrapped around the gun at the same time Vitoria's did. We each pulled and fought for it. I wrapped my index finger around the trigger. Pushing the gun barrel toward her face, I squeezed.

Vitoria jerked. Her eyes flashed fear for the first time. Blood bubbled from a hole in her neck. I fell back, exhausted, body and soul.

# CHAPTER 53

I DON'T REMEMBER THE ride to the hospital or the doctor wrapping my ribs. I don't remember Mandy yelling at me for being so stupid as to go and get myself kidnapped again, or Solomon kissing me on the forehead and telling me I'd done a good job and he was proud of me.

I was just glad to be alive. It hurt to breathe, it hurt to move, and it hurt even worse to laugh—which Mandy tried to make me do at every opportunity, because she was evil like that.

"God, Mandy, stop making me laugh. Please, you're killing me." I was lying in bed in our hotel room and had sworn to stay off my feet for a few days. Solomon was fiddling with the TV and Mandy was acting crazy.

"I'm not trying to make you laugh, but you do laugh at just about anything."

"It's the drugs," I said and took a bite of pudding. I had one arm in a sling. Eating was a bit of a challenge.

Solomon sat on the edge of the bed and I winced. "Sorry." He got up hastily.

"It's okay—just hurts to move." I reached out my good arm and took his hand. "So you're not above slipping tracking devices into my pocket?"

This time, I got an expression of surprise out of him. "You knew?"

"Of course," I said. "Why else would I let you hug me when you smelled like garbage?"

He snorted. "Yeah, so, you can never have too many backups."

"As a computer guru, I say a hearty 'amen' to that," Mandy said.

I was looking forward to getting out tomorrow, even if it was only for a walk. The FBI was covering our hotel and flight home as my fee for consulting. However, Dan was now calling me about every ten minutes, asking when I'd be back at work.

Lili was the Blonde who made it out alive, and she was in custody. I knew there had to be a mastermind behind all of it, an outside man. Lili confirmed it, but she didn't know who it was. All she'd said was that Vitoria had flown to the States every couple of months to meet someone. "So as far as we know," I said, "Vitoria is the mastermind and the girls thought they were selling their stock to a buyer in South Africa."

"You can't stop thinking about this, can you?" Mandy said.

"Well, I've been out of it, and some things are still fuzzy."

Solomon popped open a mineral water and took a drink. "Lili said that something changed six weeks ago, a new buyer or something, because Vitoria started acting strange and then the killing began. The kills were all by Vitoria. The others stood by, and everyone was too scared of her to do anything."

"Can we trace her phone? See if we can track down the buyer and the boss?"

Solomon nodded. "Doing it as we speak. Chances are that if we follow the money, we'll find them. But this is just a small operation. Most of these outfits have small hubs like this one and the rest deal in human trafficking and drugs."

I wondered if that's the path the Blondes had started down. It was only a matter of time before they went from stolen watches and credit cards to moving girls and drugs.

Taking another spoonful of pudding, I thought about Emilia. If anyone had a chance to get out and start over, it was her. I told Mandy and Solomon that I was tired and could use a nap, so they went out to go shopping. I gave Solomon props for taking my best friend shopping. He would survive and achieve knighthood in my book, or run away and forever be a martyr.

When I was alone, I closed my eyes and the tears came. I was so overwhelmed with mixed emotions that I didn't know what to think or how to feel. Her eyes—I could still see them—the life slowly trickling from her body.

Vitoria was a murderer. How were we different? I had no intention of ending a life when I walked into the warehouse. But I had killed people. Where was the line drawn? And how could I see it before it was too late?

My shoulders shook with sobs and I hoped I wasn't twisting into something I wasn't, like Vitoria had. I had to stay strong. I had to stay me. I couldn't let that dark side take control ever again.

# CHAPTER 54

THAT EVENING, SOLOMON CAME up to my room dressed in a suit and holding a red rose. He handed it to me and leaned down to kiss me. I looked like the bride of Frankenstein on a bad hair day, but he didn't seem to notice or care.

"You are one of a kind, Sarah Steele. I thought just one rose would do—any more would not say what I really want to say."

I flashed him a smile, holding my breath. "And what is it you really want to say?"

He sat down in a chair and scooted it closer to the bed. "Sarah, from the first day I met you, and from the moment you picked up that gun ..." He laughed, and I had a dumb perma-grin on my face. "I knew you were different. And you know what? I like you—I like you a lot. I can't think of anyone else I'd like to be around, so if you feel the same way, I would love it if you would be my official girlfriend."

Memories and old fears flooded to the surface, but I shoved them down. For once, I listened to the lighter side of me, the optimistic voice.

Besides, if Solomon really was the enemy... What did they say? Keep your friends close and your enemies closer. This guy was one who would be nice to hold close.

"I would love that, Solomon. Do I need to sign any paperwork, you know, to make it all official?"

He chuckled and leaned down. He gently kissed my neck, nibbled my ear, and made his way to my mouth.

No, it wouldn't be bad to keep this man close at all.

# CHAPTER 55

THE NEXT DAY AT our hotel, Mandy and I were getting ready for a day of sun and something served in a coconut.

She stuck her head out of the bathroom, mascara wand in hand. "Hey, so you remember when you told me to look into Eddie Lofton's financials?"

I was attempting to dress myself. Even though my sling was off, my ribs were really tender.

"Yeah, you find out anything?" I'd totally forgotten about it after all that had happened.

"I'm not sure, but there is something very strange going on with his records."

I walked into the bathroom. "And?"

"He wired fifty thousand dollars to an account in Norway, which isn't that strange considering he has a cousin who lives there."

I raised my eyebrows. "Geez, you went through his life with a lice comb."

"I do research the right way," Mandy said. "And thanks. Anyway, this money wire went to an offshore shipping company which has a local branch here in Rio."

"Sooo?"

"That facility is where you and the Blondes had your little showdown. Oh, and guess where this shipping company gets all its money from?"

My gut balled up, and I had a bad feeling I knew all too well. "Williams," I whispered with one eyebrow raised.

"Yeah, the one and only. So that means Eddie paid Williams Inc. and he didn't want to be connected with it, hence the ring around the rosie."

"Are you sure?"

"Yup, data doesn't lie. It's all on my laptop."

"Fifty K—the going rate for a decent hit job these days. Do you know what this means?"

"It means we should talk to Eddie." Mandy stopped, her eyes growing sad. "He must've hired Vitoria to kill his wife."

# CHAPTER 56

I BLINKED SLOWLY, AS if in a dream. The soft white comforter pillowed around me and I felt warm and at home. Every muscle had melted into the bed. I felt attached, as if I couldn't move if I tried.

The window was open. The cool sea breeze and the smell of sweet flowers wafted in.

Gradually craning my neck to the side, I looked at the time.

Ten o'clock.

I had done it. I had slept in for the first time since college.

This vacation was officially a success.

WE PACKED UP AND went over the room one last time, making sure we'd grabbed everything. "So, Mandy, we didn't get to everything on your list." I made a pouty face.

"That's okay—the list was more like a guideline, anyway. You were right—I'd make a terrible mom to a street kid." She smiled her big, sparkly, full-of-life smile. "We got to surf and talk to parrots and solve mysteries, and even stop a few criminals." She dusted off her hands and I smiled. "Not a bad vacation at all."

"I got to sleep in, so I'm happy."

"You're easy to please."

As I followed her out the door, wheeling my suitcase, I swept the room with my eyes one last time. My eye caught on something and I stopped. The light reflected on something in the air vent next to the desk. I knelt and peered into the metal grate.

"Would you look at that …" Taking two pens from my purse, I used them like chopsticks to grab what had fallen between the slats— Mandy's dragon bracelet.

I smiled. I guess not every mystery had something twisted behind it. And I was glad of that.

*Don't miss the next book in the Sarah Steele Thriller series:*

MELTING
STEELE

## ABOUT THE AUTHOR:

AARON IS THE FATHER of three kids: Soleil, Kale, and Klayton. He is the author of the bestselling Mark Appleton thriller series, The Airel Saga, and The Sarah Steele thriller series. Aaron worked in the construction field for 11 years and is now a full time writer. Aaron was home schooled and has a bachelor's degree in theology. He loves to hike, snowboard, camp, and drink coconut lattes. He is also the founder of StoneHouse Ink and Co-founder of StoneHouse University. He speaks all over the country on the subject of eBooks, writing and the changing publishing world.

Connect with Aaron at his blog: http://theworstbookever.blogspot.com

Friend him on Facebook: www.facebook.com/aaronpatterson

And Twitter: @mstcrsmith

Aaron also has a newsletter and you can get updates on his new books and way cool deals. Now you will not get bugged with a ton of emails, just when a new book comes out and such. You can sign up here: http://eepurl.com/tQWHb